open
court

open
court

Carol Clippinger

ALFRED A. KNOPF

NEW YORK

THIS IS A BORZOI BOOK PUBLISHED BY ALFRED A. KNOPF

Published in the United States by Alfred A. Knopf, an imprint of Random House Children's Books, a division of Random House, Inc., New York.

KNOPF, BORZOI BOOKS, and the colophon are registered trademarks of Random House, Inc.

www.randomhouse.com/kids

Educators and librarians, for a variety of teaching tools, visit us at www.randomhouse.com/teachers

Library of Congress Cataloging-in-Publication Data
Clippinger, Carol.
Open court / Carol Clippinger. — 1st ed.
    p.   cm.
SUMMARY: A thirteen-year-old tennis prodigy grapples with her seemingly incompatible desires to be an exceptional athlete and a normal teenager.
ISBN 978-0-375-84049-4 (trade) — ISBN 978-0-375-94049-1 (lib. bdg.)
[1. Tennis—Fiction.] I. Title.
PZ7.C62283Op 2007
[Fic]—dc22
2006024250

Printed in the United States of America

June 2007

10 9 8 7 6 5 4 3 2 1

First Edition

For my mom

open
court

• Chapter One •

I don't want to sound like I'm bragging or anything, because I'm not. Honest. Everyone's good at something. For me, it's tennis. I play on the junior circuit and travel to all sorts of tennis tournaments to compete. I usually win. I want to turn pro eventually. My friends think I've got it made. But expectations creep under my skin like soldiers, taking my brain hostage, demanding I conquer or crumble.

Tennis ruins my feet. Makes them ugly. The stop-start motions and side-to-side movements of the sport breed blisters. They plague me, attack my soft flesh. I always keep a small box full of blister treatments with my tennis gear.

All athletes have rituals, game day or not. Some eat the same carb-loaded breakfast every morning or have specific sports drinks nearby at all times; others wear lucky underwear or socks. Me? I wouldn't dream of leaving the house without popping my blisters first. Especially today, with this infected blister.

First I placed a towel under the offending foot. (My mom doesn't want blister puss on her carpet. Who can blame her? It's gross.) One click of a lighter produced a perfect oval flame. I sterilized the needle by roasting it in the middle of the heat. Clenching my teeth, squinting, I forced it in, piercing the flesh before I lost my nerve.

Puss oozed immediately. Ooze is the worst. Hate the ooze. I applied pressure to the opposite end to let the puss trickle out until only a white pocket of empty skin remained. For the moment I placed a Band-Aid over the empty pocket. I'd drain it again before practice.

Coach yells if I show up for practice with an untreated blister. Even when drained they make me walk tender. A delicate gait isn't allowed in tennis. Ever.

"Quit limping. It doesn't hurt that bad," Coach always says. "Suck it up and be a man."

"But, Coach, I'm a girl."

"No excuses. It's only pain, get over it."

I pressed my hand on top of the Band-Aid to let the

heat from my fingers ease the throb underneath. It'd feel better in a minute.

There isn't much to do in Colorado Springs, Colorado. That's probably the conclusion of anyone who has lived their entire life in one place, like I have. After a while boredom sets in and suffocates me. But today was the first day of summer vacation and my possibilities were wide open. I put my blister remedies away and headed down the street to Melissa's house.

I'd rather have hung out with Eve, my best friend, but she was gone for the day. Melissa was never my first choice because she was a few years younger than Eve and I. There weren't any kids her age in the neighborhood, so she was pathetically grateful for our friendship. She had the sad eyes and constant whine of a lost puppy. Most of the time her clothes didn't match, and she didn't even care.

Melissa O'Donnell often solved our hunger problems. She was one of five kids, and her mom probably spent a thousand dollars a week at the grocery store. I'm not kidding. Opening the O'Donnell refrigerator was a religious experience. It was crammed with brand-name junk food, free for the taking. I can honestly say I've never spent time at Melissa's without eating something. Melissa didn't really mind, though. We never asked for food, she *offered* it. I can't really say no to a free Snickers bar—who can?

Three houses away from Melissa's I spotted a girl drowning a lilac bush in her front yard. I recognized her from school. We'd never spoken.

"You going to Melissa's?" she called.

I'm not a person who enjoys dumb questions from people I don't know. I wondered if I should answer or pretend I didn't hear her hollow voice and keep on walking. I paused for half a second and took another step.

"You going to Melissa's?" she said again.

I faced her. "Yeah."

"I know Melissa," she said, dropping the hose.

I took a few steps toward her; she took a few toward me. "Oh yeah?" I said.

"I'm Polly Cassini," she said.

"I'm Hall Braxton. Did you just move here?"

"Yeah, we've been here two months. Used to live in Briargate. We just finished unpacking. I've seen you and Melissa and that other girl—"

"Eve?"

"Yeah, Eve—walking together," she said.

"Oh."

We watched water spill out of the round garden hose opening and creep into blades of grass. The thirsty earth

4

underneath quickly sucked it in. I hate talking to people I don't know; I can never think of anything to say until the conversation is finished. I'm quite articulate after the fact.

"Melissa's mom just got back from the grocery store," Polly said, her brown hair flying in the wind. "Got home, like, five minutes ago. I saw her carrying the bags from the car. I counted thirteen."

"Thirteen bags?"

"Bet she bought ice cream. And Red Hots, too. They have gobs of Red Hots."

I smiled. "They have cans of Coke, not two-liter bottles. Cans are the best."

She grabbed my sleeve, suddenly eager. "I could use a snack," she said. "What are we waiting for?"

We walked, with purpose, the short distance to Melissa's. I snuck a glance at Polly. She wasn't pretty, exactly, but her face was interesting. Pouty cheeks. Small earlobes. A chameleon; she could be a lot of different things if she chose. My face wasn't as generic as hers, which could be good or bad, I wasn't sure. A wave of déjà vu swept over me, like I knew this girl from somewhere, but where?

"I'm not eating anything," I proclaimed. It was wrong to use Melissa this way, even if she didn't mind.

"Yeah, sure," Polly said.

"I'm serious."

"You'll cave."

Polly rang the bell. *Ding-dong.*

Melissa opened the door and grinned like it was Easter and we were the bunny. "Hey, you guys know each other?"

"We just met," Polly said. "Can you hang out?"

"I gotta put the groceries away first," Melissa said.

"No problem. We'll help," Polly offered, gliding inside. She pretended to be sly, but I could tell she wasn't there for the food—she liked Melissa. Her tone of voice was affectionate.

We sat on the kitchen counter while Melissa shoved groceries into cupboards. She didn't want help, only our company.

"Don't you have tennis practice today?" Melissa asked me.

"Not till later." The last thing I wanted to talk about was tennis. Leave it to Melissa to bring it up.

"You play tennis?" Polly asked.

"Tell her all the stuff you won."

"It's no big deal," I said.

"What'd you win?" Polly asked, curious now. She shoveled a fistful of Red Hots into her mouth.

"Tell her what you won."

"I got to the semifinals of the United States Tennis Association National Open in Utah, and won the Junior Orange Bowl the last two years. Won the Great Pumpkin Sectional Championship, did well at the Columbus Indoors. It goes for a while—stop me anytime."

Polly shrugged.

"She's a nationally ranked player," Melissa said. "Ranked number one in all of America, right, Hall?"

"I'm not number one," I protested.

"What number are you?" Polly asked.

"I'm number four in the USTA, Junior Division, Girls 14's—I'm thirteen, but Girls 14's includes thirteen- and fourteen-year-olds."

Melissa nodded. "That means only three other girls in the whole world are better."

"No. It means in the *United States,* in my *age group,* only three other girls are better. An international ranking is more important. You have to play foreign tournaments to get one, starting when you're thirteen. I've only played one so far—in Mexico. I lost."

"Yeah, but her coach used to pay the Cheyenne Mountain boys' tennis team to hit with her. She kept winning. Now they don't want to play her anymore. Isn't that right, Hall?" Melissa said.

"You beat high school boys? No way!"

7

"Jeez, Melissa. Do you have to tell her everything?"

"No way!" Polly said again. She looked at Melissa, then me, trying to decipher if we were playing a prank.

"Can we talk about something else?" I said.

"You don't like it, do you?" Polly asked.

"Like what?"

"Tennis. You hate it," Polly said.

"I don't hate anything," I protested.

"OK," Polly said like she didn't believe me. "Whatever you say."

"I'm saying I don't hate tennis."

"OK."

I've been a "prodigy," a "tennis phenomenon," since I picked up a racquet at age six. That's what my dad says, anyway. It's probably what lots of fathers say about their kids' abilities, except in my case it's true. As my dad puts it, I "hit the hell out of the ball."

Tennis is what I do. It's who I am.

My coach, Trent, says I'm so good it *hurts* to watch me. But my talent, and trophies, and crap I've won are starting to backfire. There isn't any competition left within my region: I play the same twenty girls over and over. Sometimes I "play up" in tournaments, against sixteen-year-olds, and win. Without competition my game won't improve.

Suddenly I'm a problem, concern, difficulty. My parents are considering sending me to live at a tennis academy to advance my tennis career. They say it's the next step for me to turn pro. The Bickford Tennis Academy—in *Florida*—is high on their list.

Tennis academies turn tennis talent into tennis legend. Academy kids live in dorms and attend private school four hours a day. The rest of their day is devoted to tennis, cross-training, and more tennis. Homework gets completed in the wee hours of the morning, apparently.

Academies are particular about who they let in. Only the top players survive. Tennis doesn't have the same age restrictions as other professional sports. Girls as young as *fifteen* turn pro. The younger, the better.

Most tennis academy kids won't end up turning pro, but they'll at least get a full athletic scholarship to Harvard, Notre Dame, or Stanford. The best that can happen—the goal—is that a kid will turn pro and start raking in serious amounts of cash on the ATP or WTA tour. This happens maybe two percent of the time. *Two percent.* I know, I've read the statistics.

These adults that claim to love me, my own flesh and blood, might be sending me away to live at an academy. The thought of it makes me sick. I'm a champion in Colorado. At a place like Bickford Tennis Academy everyone is a champion. Maybe better than me. At Bickford I might be the worst player. Worst of the best. It's not worth the risk. I want to stay in Colorado, be coached by my own coach, and win. I'm a champion here. Why would I want to go anywhere else?

"The only thing I'm good at is math," Polly said, returning my thoughts back to the real world. "I hate math."

"I'm good at piano," Melissa offered.

My promise not to eat was short-lived. Without thinking, I dug my hand into a bag of pretzels and popped several into my mouth. Polly raised an eyebrow at me as I chewed. I shrugged. She smiled.

"I gotta get going," she said, glancing at her watch. She thanked Melissa profusely for the Red Hots.

"Want to ride bikes, Hall?" Melissa asked.

I had nothing better to do. Tennis practice didn't start for another couple of hours. "OK. I'll go get my bike. Meet me halfway?"

"Sure," she said.

I pressed my back against the O'Donnells' screen door and clicked the latch open with one perfect jab of my elbow.

"Bye, Melissa," Polly chirped.

"Later," Melissa said.

The screen door slammed. Polly and I stepped out clutching cans of root beer. The wind collided with my skin and crept up my spine. Polly hummed a few lines of "The Star-Spangled Banner" while watching a fluorescent grasshopper jump across the sidewalk. The girl was an oddity: plain on the outside but exotic in spirit.

"Crap!" She seized my shoulder. "I forgot the water! Can you turn the hose off on the way up? I'll be late," she said sweetly, like I might say no if she didn't coat it with sugar. "I go to math camp in the afternoons," she explained. "Can't miss the bus."

"Why?"

"Why can't I miss—"

"No, why math camp?"

"So I can be brilliant." She giggled at the thought and pushed her bangs out of her eyes. She stood stiff, waiting for me to dismiss her or something.

"Um . . . Melissa and Eve and I hang out at Eve's all summer long. Like, every day. You can come if you want."

I'd made her day. "Really?"

I nodded. "Sure."

She backed up, ready to run. "The hose—you'll turn it off?"

I nodded. "Bye."

I was mildly amused when half a minute later I found myself in the mud, crouched down like a chimpanzee, to cut the water supply. I had known this Polly girl for less than twenty minutes and she already had me doing her a favor.

• Chapter Two •

"All right, warrior, how does it feel to win?"

"Hmmm?"

"Don't play dumb with me."

My coach, Trent, and I sat in his office at the country club. He loomed behind his massive desk. I lay like a dishrag on the couch, ready to die from muscle aches. My mom was late picking me up from practice, so I'd decided to hang out and bug Trent. It was more like he was bugging me.

I rolled my eyes to irk him. "It feels nice," I said.

"Well, that's a load of crap."

Coach questions me at unsuspecting moments to see if my thoughts toward the game are pure. I'm a warrior and I'm supposed to think like one. It gives him pleasure to crack open my head and rearrange things. If painting my stick (players call their racquets sticks when off court) bright orange would make me win, I'd be forced to comply. Mostly I give in and see things his way.

"Come on, Coach, I'm tired. Even my eyeballs hurt."

"Practice hasn't ended until you answer the question."

"You threatening me?"

"Yes."

Trent is simply huge. Muscles ripple from his tall frame like large smooth rocks. His deep voice is packed with authority. His skin is the color of chocolate. Lots of people, I can tell, are afraid of him.

"OK, OK, um, when I win it feels like my feet have wings. The tennis balls are as big as coconuts coming over the net. Can't miss. I have no fear."

"How does it feel to lose?"

"Sucks."

"Explain."

Coach knows it rattles my cage when I lose. Champions, when they lose, are *supposed* to be upset, but it doesn't simply upset me, it makes me go berserk. Girls who *always* lose don't have to worry about pressure. No one expects them to win. Sometimes I'd prefer to be them—they get to go home early and rest their aching flesh. I can't say that to Trent, though, the man will behead me, so I tell him what he wants to hear.

I cleared my throat. "Losing sucks worse than anything. When I lose, my legs are so heavy it feels like I'm wearing cement shoes. Easy shots become difficult and it's my fault entirely. Losing equals fear."

"So you'd rather . . ."

"Win."

He sipped his iced tea and studied my face, looking for sincerity. He wasn't talking *to* me about tennis, he was talking *at* me. "What are you?"

"You should start a cult or something. You could have players across America reciting your mantra on demand."

He wiped nonexistent dust off the top of his beloved, case-enclosed, signed Roger Maris baseball while pretending to be offended. "They laughed at Noah, too, until it rained."

"Coach, come on, I'm tired. Can't I sit here without being grilled?"

"No. What are you?"

I sighed. "A warrior."

"What do you do?"

"Play tennis."

"Who wins?" he demanded.

"I do."

"Who has a better fitness level, you or Kim Clijsters?"

Kim Clijsters was a Belgian top-ten pro player whose athleticism was stunning. I'd seen her do the *splits* on court when running down a ball and still hit a winner.

"I do."

"Who's got better focus out there, you or Maria Sharapova?"

Maria Sharapova was a six-foot-tall pro Russian whose focus never wavered. The girl could be down two match points and manage to squeak out a win.

"My focus is better."

"And when you turn pro who are you going to blast off that court the first chance you get?"

"Kim Clijsters and Maria Sharapova."

"When you're losing what do you do?"

"Find a way to win."

His jaw relaxed into a smile. As always, he'd won our battle of wills.

"My mom is probably here by now," I said, gathering my tennis bag. "I'll see you tomorrow."

"Working on your serves tonight?"

"As soon as I get home."

"Good girl. Think big, you'll be big."

"See you, Coach."

The Country Club of Colorado is different from the

real world—harsher somehow. I tried befriending club girls in the past but it never worked. Most were snobs. The only reason I'm allowed at the club at all is because Trent works here. He finagled free access for me in exchange for my tournament trophies being displayed at the club. My accomplishments are often used as a bartering chip. Sad but true.

I walked down the air-conditioned stairwell into the clubhouse lobby. Exactly fifty-eight steps bring me to the club's front entrance; the fifty-ninth spits me out the door and into the parking lot. My mom waited in her usual spot, illegally parked in front of a fire hydrant.

My mom and dad don't involve themselves in my tennis activities. They don't go to practices and rarely have time to go to tournaments. They never ask if I've won or lost. My mom only says, "Did you have fun, honey?" My dad says, "Was the umpire fair?" That's it. Once in a while, when they find out I've really clobbered someone, my dad's face breaks into an obnoxious smile. Then my mom jabs her elbow into his ribs and he's quick to let his face straighten. My parents want me to think they love me because I'm their daughter, not because I win tournaments.

But lately when they find out I've won against a difficult girl or that my ranking has gone up *again*, they act weird. My dad suddenly takes the whole family to

Baskin-Robbins for ice cream. Lets us order anything we want; he never does that. Then my mom surprises me with a subscription to *Tennis* magazine—without me asking.

I'm kind of suspicious, paranoid, ill over things like ice cream and magazine subscriptions. I wonder if all kids get paid off like this before they get shipped off to slave tennis academies.

I hopped in the front seat and threw my bag in back. My mom floored the gas and within seconds we were headed home.

"I've got to meet your dad in forty minutes, so I'm going to drop you off at the practice court on the way."

"But it's nearly seven o'clock. I'm starving."

Keeping her eyes on the road, she rummaged through her huge purse, producing a ham sandwich wrapped in plastic and a warm bottle of Evian. "Dinner is served," she said.

"I ate a ham sandwich for lunch."

"If we had a stove in the car I'd make you something else."

"Why can't I go home and walk to the court after I eat real food?"

My mom sighed. "Honey, don't complain. I'm saving you from walking six blocks. I don't have the energy to argue. It's not going to kill you to eat a ham sandwich."

18

Silence.

"Your dad doesn't have to work tonight. I snuck out of work early so I could drop you off and meet him on time for once. Don't argue."

"OK."

My dad works a second job at night to pay for my coaching. Trent isn't a hack who only knows the basics; he's a real coach. He develops talent, nurtures abilities. He's molded me into a player. Developing, nurturing, and molding cost piles of cash.

She pulled the car to the side of the court. "See you at home," she said.

"Bye," I said, taking a bite of my sandwich.

"Michael and Brad should be here soon. Don't walk home alone."

"Yeah, OK."

"Hall?" my mom said as I got out and started to shut the car door. "Did you talk to Trent about Janie yet?"

My mouth got dry. "Yes," I lied. I stared at the zipper of my tennis bag.

"What did he say? Is he going to take you to see Janie?"

I stared at her, exhausted. My mom is the Essence of Momness—the type who makes sure I have lunch money and says the right thing when I'm sad. I know she wants to protect me from the crisis that's happened

19

to my old doubles partner, Janie Alessandro. But there is no protection. And I think I know that more than she does. Still, Janie is our undercurrent of tension, the lump in our throats, her plight fresh in our minds.

"Hall, what did Trent say?"

"He said a lot of stuff, Mom. I told you before. I don't want to talk about it with you. You barely knew Janie."

"And you don't have to talk about it—to me. But are you talking about it to Trent?"

"Yes, I talked to him," I lied again. "I'm OK about it, I swear," I said. Two lies in less than two minutes; that must be a record. I didn't want to think about how poor Janie had been ruined by tennis, much less discuss it.

"All right, Hall. You know I'm here if you want to talk," she said, her thumb tapping the steering wheel.

"I know," I said. "See you."

"Have a good practice, honey."

As I took a step toward the court déjà vu nudged me again. *Polly*. Her joy and ample cheeks—those were Janie's traits. *That's* why she seemed so familiar. No wonder I liked her.

I practice my serves in the dark. This old court is six blocks from my house. It's across from the Benet Hill Center, which used to be a monastery. No one except me plays here. The court backs up to the bluffs and the nearby street is quiet—great for practice. The gate is padlocked, but around back there's a place in the fence wide enough to shimmy through. The court itself is in terrible shape. Weeds grow out of its cracked surface. The windscreen is all but ripped off. I don't mind, though. It's the only court within walking distance.

Yesterday I rigged the sagging net with duct tape and heavy string to get it back to the regulation three feet. The right net height is important when I practice serves.

My parents don't want me out after dark because they're afraid I'll get kidnapped or something. My brothers, Michael and Brad, are supposed to walk me to the court at seven-thirty, then walk me home around nine-thirty. This thrills them in a way I can't express. The idea (my mom's) was that they'd ride bikes or play street hockey with their friends outside the court while I practiced. That's not what happens, though. They ditch me the minute the court is in sight and don't return until well after dark.

Protecting me is not high on my brothers' list of priorities. But I never tell on them—I prefer to practice alone.

I usually warm up by hitting against the backboard. Then I move on to serves. At dusk they're precise. By the time darkness rests on the court I'm close to perfection. The wobbling court light still works. It flickers on automatically, causing my body to cast a huge, ominous shadow. I look eight feet tall. An Amazon armed with a racquet.

I practice half my serves with my eyes closed. Coach taught me how. Serving blind allows me to *feel* the serve instead of *thinking* the serve. Makes me trust myself rather than trying to bargain the ball inside the lines. Trent says there's no bargaining in tennis, only trust. His voice is inside my head guiding me as I hit each shot.

. . . take it on the rise . . .

. . . hustle, hustle . . .

. . . extend racquet . . .

. . . chip and charge, chip and charge . . .

I step to the baseline and look across the barren court. I see myself as Trent sees me; I am a warrior who hurls Penn balls over the net and crushes the bones of my weaker opponent. In the darkness each move I make is larger, bigger, more. Every shuffle of feet and turn of shoulder echoes of glory. The Penn balls throb with beauty.

I love this game.

Mentally, I let go of the barriers of my limits until I think of nothing. A blank head is where perfection rests. It's how I hear Coach's voice. It's how I get in the zone.

. . . thump . . .

. . . thump . . .

Stepping outside my flesh, I wait for each flawless hit to perfect me. Here I am not someone's little sister. Not someone's daughter. Not someone's friend. This game beckons me—chooses me. I am a warrior. An Amazon. I am beautiful. And I play to win.

I place my tennis shoes an inch from the baseline. Holding a ball and racquet, my hands are side by side. Slowly I separate them. As the ball floats upward, I move my racquet back. In one seamless motion my feet leave the ground and I force the strings to make contact with the yellow ball. My entire body, every cell in my body, hits the ball and brings it to life as it crosses the net.

. . . thump . . .

I open my eyes to see if it was positioned in the service court the way I intended. It was.

That's my typical practice: focused, intense, exhilarating.

But today as I unloaded my gear, the court looked amiss, as if it'd doubled in size. I wasn't sure why, but I felt different, too, like I'd shrunk a few inches. No matter. All I had to do was step to the baseline and invite the excellence in. I'd done it a million times. Racquet in my grip, I let the calm pour over me like water. Squeezing a

Penn ball in my left hand, I made my muscles contract in sync with my heartbeat. I waited for Trent's voice to bubble up from my guts and into my head to guide my shots.

Hmmm . . . I couldn't hear him for some reason. I stopped squeezing the ball. And waited. I quieted my breathing. And waited. Still, my guts weren't bubbling. Hmmm. I closed my eyes, bowed my head slightly, listening . . . listening . . . I felt a light rumble, mumble, in my belly. It was Coach's voice, finally, but the volume was so low I couldn't decipher his commands. Hmmm.

I bounced up and down, waking my feet. Quickly I tossed the ball and slammed my racquet into it. Out. Anyone can mishit. No big deal.

Again. Toss. Slam the ball. Out.

Come on, Hall, I told myself. *It's a serve to no one. Get it right!*

Again. Toss. Racquet back. Extend racquet. Hit it lightly. Nice and easy. Can't miss this one.

But I did.

Trent's voice is a part of my game. Makes me win. My guts churned, writhed, twisted. I felt light-headed.

"Trent?" I said weakly.

Fear exploded in my belly. The court spun around and around. Bile backed up in my throat. Dropping to the court, I put my palms on the green surface, hoping to regain balance. Suddenly the thought of Bickford Tennis Academy seized my brain and scared the bejesus out of me.

I tried shaking it off. Maybe I was sick. Maybe I had the flu or food poisoning. Damn ham sandwich.

"Trent?" I said softly. The small mumble of his voice ceased altogether, choked by my fear.

I shoved my gear into my bag, sat with my back against the fence, and waited for Michael and Brad. I knew I couldn't tell anyone about this. If I did, it'd probably freak them out big-time.

• Chapter Three •

Eve Jensen's house is two blocks away, an easy jog downhill. It's a redbrick house landscaped with an aspen tree and barrels of spring flowers, identical to the rest of the houses along Wynkoop Drive.

Eve's parents are divorced, and with just her and her mom living there, her house is filled with lace curtains, flowery comforters, and rose potpourri. Void of sports equipment, dirty socks, and ESPN, it's nothing like my house. Her mom works, so we have the house to ourselves five days a week.

Eve Jensen has been my best friend since our first day of kindergarten. We just hit it off. We're complete opposites, though. With her sturdy frame, blond hair, and eyes the color of the sky, she looks like an export from Norway. Aside from her light coloring, her face is largely about her nose and its four freckles, which she detests. My hair is the color of mud, as are my eyes. I'm tall but thin. My mom calls me a wisp of a girl.

Melissa opened the screen door. "Hey, Hall, what took you so long? Eve's making cookies."

"I got here as soon as I—oh no . . ."

Melissa took a handful of cookie dough and smeared it down my bare arm, slightly petrified of the retaliation she'd face.

"Want some?" she taunted innocently.

Sometimes we made cookies the normal way—with an oven—and sometimes we didn't. The batter was inexplicably better than the baked cookie. I scraped dough from my arm, kneading it, deciding who to ambush. Inside, doubled over with laughter, Eve was an easy target.

"Think it's funny, do you?" I lunged toward her.

"No, no, nooo . . ." She tried to run.

"Ha!" I slapped a generous helping on the back of her sunburned neck. "Got you!"

But Eve quickly held her hand out, knowing I'd back into it, and coated my leg with mush. "Agg!"

Eve got hysterical with laughter. Hyena screeches echoed through the kitchen.

I nodded to Melissa. I started chanting, "Attack, attack, attack!"

"Attack, attack, attack!" Melissa joined in.

I emptied the bowl of cookie dough. Grinning, with two handfuls of ammunition, I took revenge. Eve backed up, cornered by the couch.

"No, no!" she wailed. "Stop!"

Her cries were in vain. Melissa fell to the floor, face purple with laughter, grateful it wasn't her. Eve responded as if tortured. "I'm gonna pee, I'm gonna pee!"

It was a popular phrase for Eve whenever things got tense. I considered it an accomplishment any time I managed to squeeze those three words out of her.

"I'm gonna pee . . . *I'm gonna pee!*" she screeched.

I wished for the moment she would lose control and spontaneously pee. That'd be a riot. She hadn't yet, but there was always hope.

I was both sucking some cookie batter from my thumb and dislodging a chocolate chip from my thigh when Polly bounded through Eve's screen door.

"You made cookies without me?" she said, surveying the damage. "No fair. Chocolate chip is my favorite."

"Sorry," Melissa said. "Maybe next time."

Polly nodded. "That's what I get for being late. Oh, guess who rode past me on their bikes."

"Who?" Eve asked.

"That guy you all love, Luke Kimberlin, and his friend, um, that Bruce Weissman guy."

Luke Kimberlin was the Greek god our thirteen-year-old existence revolved around. Polly had been sufficiently filled in on the saga.

"They did not," I said.

"Oh yes they did," Polly sang. "I saw them."

"Did Luke talk to you?" I asked.

"No," Polly said, "but he almost looked my way."

"Almost doesn't count," Eve said, touching the end of her nose, covering three out of four freckles.

"Where does he go to school again?" Polly asked.

"Westland Prep. It's a fancy private school," I said. "So Luke is gorgeous, smart, *and* rich."

"He got suspended from Westland last month for spraying cans of whipped cream onto the vice principal's new car. It stained the paint," Eve said.

Polly fluffed up her bangs and pushed them out of the way. "He *did not.*"

"Yes he did," I said.

"Now I'm hungry for an ice cream sundae," Melissa announced. "With whipped cream."

We burst out laughing.

Polly looked enviously at the cookie dough I ate. "Really, you should've waited for me," she moaned, still upset.

Melissa scraped some spare dough from the bowl and smeared it on Polly's arm. "There you go," she said.

As we gathered in Eve's kitchen, Polly turned to me and asked the question that everyone eventually asks. "What's your real name?"

"Hall is my real name," I sighed. "Actually, Holloway."

"Holloway *Louise* Braxton," Eve helped.

"Everybody calls me Hall."

"Hall," Polly said, like I was a thing, not a person.

"You know, kitchen . . . living room . . . hall."

"It's a family name," Eve said in my defense.

Polly winced lightly. "I like it," she lied.

"You don't have to like it. Sometimes it even gives me a headache, and it's my name," I said, yawning.

"Her name should be Foghorn, she snores so loud," Eve said.

Polly laughed. "Maren snores so loud her boyfriend has nightmares of a train running him over. He's got sensitive ears. Last week my brother, Teddy, and I had the TV on so low we practically had to read David Letterman's lips and it still woke him."

"Who is Maren?" I asked.

"My mom," Polly said. "Somehow 'Mom' doesn't fit her."

"How long has your mom been dating the guy?" Eve asked.

"Since New Year's. Maren was at a party, and Pete—that's his name—Pete spilled punch on her shoes. When midnight came around he said the least he could do was kiss her. Isn't that romantic?" Polly gushed.

"Enough chitchat," Eve said. "Are we bike riding or what?"

It was no surprise that while I still had hunks of dough on me, Eve looked freshly scrubbed. She did everything fast: walking, eating, sucking cookie dough from her elbow. She liked being first.

"It's two o'clock," Polly said. "Gotta go to math camp. Sorry."

"We'll walk you," I said.

Eve groaned.

We escorted Polly three blocks to the decrepit bus stop. Eve kept our pace brisk, walking a half step ahead while attempting to rub the freckles off her nose.

Polly offered us a weak smile as she scaled the bus steps, as if it was OK she had to spend her summer doing math problems while we remained free. Could anything be worse? She was a good actress; I had to admit it. She tapped the window, saying goodbye.

Once the bus pulled away the dissection began. Polly was our newest friend; her peculiarities were fair game.

"She calls her mom Maren?" Eve said, wiping sweat from her brow. "What is she, thirty-five?"

"That's nothing," Melissa said. "I was at her house yesterday. Her mom said the f-word, like, five times."

"Her mom?" I asked.

"Her mom," Melissa said, "said that and a whole lot more." We'd reached Melissa's driveway. She stopped. "I can't ride bikes, either. Got a piano lesson."

"See you later, then," Eve said.

"Bye," Melissa called, and cut across her lawn.

I felt I was in a race—one I hadn't agreed to participate in. This was often my feeling with Eve and bikes. If she walked a half step ahead, she biked a full wheel ahead. She liked speed. Still, riding bikes was my favorite part of our friendship. We didn't have to talk all the time.

We rode in sweeping circles, spiraling under the sun. "We've got to find some shade—I'm cooking on this as-phalt. How about the horse stables? That whole street has tree shade," she said.

32

She'd taken horseback-riding lessons there last summer and liked biking there ever since.

"Go for it," I said.

Eve sprinted out in front, face against the hot breeze. I let her lead the way; I didn't have a choice. If I led, she pedaled so fast her front tire continually bumped my rear wheel, causing her to apologize for twenty blocks.

Despite her natural agression, Eve disliked any kind of organized sports. A bike ride was one thing, but actual games with rules and regulations bored her immensely. That, more than anything else, was the reason she was my best friend. She cared nothing about my tennis game. Because she never asked about it, I was able to get away from it completely when I was with her. She was my one respite, oasis, haven from the sport.

I wondered if my former doubles partner, Janie, would've kept her sanity if she had a friend like Eve.

We rode for nearly two miles. She stopped under the first oak tree in a row of twenty, near the dirt entrance of the stables. I raised my hair off the back of my neck, fanned my face.

"So," Eve said, "now that Melissa isn't here . . . What do you really think of Polly?"

"I like her. Don't you?"

She shrugged. "She's OK, I guess. Nothing special."

I was struck. "Nothing special? That's it?"

Eve rested her foot on her pedal. "Well, she's not you. And she's not me. It could be worse—her clothes match, so at least she's not Melissa."

"That's true. She's lucky, though, seeing Luke like that. I wish I could accidentally stumble upon him that easily."

"Yeah, that's really not fair. We had dibs on Luke first. Even Melissa would have dibs on Luke before Polly!" Eve said sarcastically. "Hey, want to swing by my house and get a drink? Even this shade is hot."

"Sure."

Eve turned her bike and pedaled, with me right behind.

It was dinnertime when I finally headed back up Wynkoop Drive to get home. As I crossed the street I saw Luke Kimberlin and Bruce pedaling their bikes toward me. Luke's wheels slowed. His shirt clung to his chest. He looked me straight in the eye. I was sure of it. I opened my mouth to say something, anything, but only air came out.

"That was the one," he said to Bruce as they passed. "What do you think?"

He was talking about me! I was the one. I had to be the one; no one else was on the street. What was I the one of? The ugly one? Stupid one? I wasn't sure. My heart was in my throat. Sailing down the street, their bikes, like magic carpets, safely transported them from my view.

• Chapter Four •

In my upstairs hallway, if I place my ear directly over the heating vent in the floor, I can clearly hear the conversation of whoever is in the kitchen. Since my parents talk about us in the kitchen, my brothers and I use this technique to our advantage: we admit guilt or feign innocence depending on what they already know.

Brad spotted my ear to the floor. "You, me, or Michael?" he asked.

"Shush. Me."

"Good," he said, and moseyed back into his room.

The conversation was definitely about me and it was going something like this:

Dad: "She's outgrown Trent."

36

Mom: "Academies are four thousand dollars a month, some of them more. Not to mention the pressure they put on those children. They're *children,* Frank, not marines. The places are run like boot camps. They look so sad."

Dad: "Ridiculous. Most are resorts—*we* should be so lucky. The facilities make Trent's coaching seem minor-league. A one-to-five teaching ratio from former pros!"

Mom: "Frank, I—"

Dad: "An academy is a springboard for the international circuit, Vivian. Junior *world* rankings. Kick the heck out of Russian girls, French girls . . . German girls." He sighed. "She'll be *challenged* instead of driving in the back of Trent's car to a Vegas tournament for the hundredth time."

Mom: "What about the pressure? I don't want her crumbling like Janie Alessandro. That's a tragedy."

Dad: "You've asked her about Janie a hundred times. She's fine with it. She won't end up like Janie Alessandro."

Mom: "How do you know?"

That was all I could hear because the dishwasher rinse cycle kicked in, flooding the vent with a gurgling ruckus.

The United States Tennis Association junior rankings are only for girls in the United States. In order to qualify for an International Tennis Federation junior ranking, which is way more important, I'd have to start playing bunches of foreign tournaments. We couldn't afford it; we could barely afford tournaments in the United States.

I know it bothered my dad. Internationally I'd be ranked much lower. International tennis is *serious* tennis.

Still, I felt renewed. My parents didn't have enough money to auction off their only daughter to a lame tennis academy. Yay for poverty! I could go to practice with an easy conscience. Yet somehow I knew they wouldn't give up that easily.

Trent stood outside his office. "Glad I caught you. I've got a meeting. Hang out for a while. Meet me at the court at one o'clock."

"Sure."

I keep a beach bag in Coach's office for times like this. No reason to wait in his office when I can be outside. After I slipped on my swimsuit, I headed to the snack bar and bought a Diet Coke (Coach doesn't want me consuming lots of sugar) and a slice of pizza. I almost made it to the pool area alive; my toe jammed into the corner of a chair leg. Bone against metal. "Ow, ouch, ouch." I seized my foot. My Diet Coke sloshed out of its container and slopped all over my white shirt. "Typical!"

As I limped to my lounge chair and wrung out my shirt, I realized how lonely practice had become without Janie around. Had she been here she'd have made fun of me for being a klutz. Janie's personality made everything lively. Shielding my eyes from the sun, I scanned the club members, hoping to see her, knowing I wouldn't.

Could it be? It was! Not Janie, but Luke Kimberlin . . . twenty feet away and fast approaching.

I grabbed a magazine and pretended to read. My toe ached something fierce. I sort of waved my foot around, hoping to ease the pain. The Greek God approached my island and stood, waiting to be adored. Kicking my lounge chair, he scooted it inches across the cement. I met his eyes and looked away with a big dumb grin on my face.

"I thought it was you," he said. "I didn't know you were a member."

Incredibly, he sat at the foot of my lounge chair. He was actually speaking to me.

"Oh, well, um . . . I'm not, really. Um, my tennis coach works here, so they let me use the courts for free."

The stain on my shirt left a question mark on his face.

"They should have lids for the cups," I said.

"Yeah," he said calmly, "they do have lids."

"I didn't see any."

"Right up there, by the straws."

"I'm sure they are, but I didn't see any."

"What happened to your toe?" he said.

"Stubbed it. It's fine."

"It's bleeding all over the cement."

"I know. It'll be OK in a minute."

He ran his fingers through his dark hair; that seemed to be a habit. Wavy strands fell perfectly back into place. His deep brown eyes were flecked with gold, making them shine in the light. His forehead looked like wealth: perfectly shaped, tan, completely zit-free. Great forehead. His beauty slapped me in the face and said, *Look at me.*

Luke's father was a doctor. They vacationed in Europe. I knew so much about him I felt like a stalker. But why was he talking to *me*? Maybe he wasn't. Maybe I was imagining this. No, it had to be real. My toe throbbed too much for it to be a daydream.

"Feels good to be out of school, huh?" he said.

"Three months of freedom."

"I was supposed to take golf lessons, but I didn't sign up in time. Now the classes are full."

"Too bad," I said.

"I'd rather swim and hang out with my friends, anyway."

"Oh . . . yeah . . . sure."

"Hey, can I borrow a dollar? I need a drink."

Oddly enough, the Greek God was panhandling money from me. I felt honored. "I just used all my cash on lunch. Sorry."

"That's OK," he said, visually surfing the crowds for other financial opportunities. He looked back at me. "Are those your tennis trophies in that glass case in the lobby?" He seemed impressed.

"You saw those?" I asked.

He nodded. "Are they yours?"

"Yes." I was at a loss as to what to say to Luke. My heart thundered. I didn't know how to talk to a boy I liked. I'd never liked anyone before now.

"That's awesome," he said.

I nodded. Luke was complimenting *me*? I needed a camera! Quick! I had to snap a photo of Luke and me together or the girls would never believe it. Everything in me wanted to stay put and see where this would go. But if I didn't head toward the courts in about five seconds, I'd be late for practice.

"My tennis practice starts right now. You can watch. If you want. I mean, since you're here," I blurted out, stunning even myself.

He glanced at his watch. "Let me grab my beach towel. I'll catch up."

"It's court three—the outside courts."

He nodded, starting a slow jog to retrieve his towel.

What luck! I slipped my shorts on over my swimsuit. Carrying my bag, I cut through the grass.

"Holloway Braxton, wait up!" He knew my last name! It sounded beautiful, angels singing my praise into the country club air.

"Coach yells if I'm late."

Luke grabbed my icy drink, his fingers against mine. "Can I?" He pressed his pink lips to the paper rim, gulping. Then he dug ice out with his fingers. "Thanks."

Trent stood waiting. The man hates waiting.

"Coach, this is Luke. Luke, this is my coach, Trent."

"Two minutes late. No time for conversation."

Luke captured the strap of my tennis bag. "Want me to take this? I'll sit on the bleachers."

My Wednesday was in full bloom. I grinned stupidly. "Hold my drink?" I asked. I took a big swig out of the cup, placing my mouth exactly where his had been, before handing it to him.

Thump . . . thump . . . thump . . .

. . . thump . . . thump . . .

I didn't have to fret about getting Trent's voice to bubble from my belly into my head. Coach's real voice plagued my eardrums from the moment practice began until it ended. Thank God.

I listened to the specific twang a tennis ball makes when it hits the racquet strings just right. I dream about this twang. This twang makes me feel beautiful even though I have hair and eyes the color of mud. Maybe Luke Kimberlin liked girls who reminded him of mud. Anything seemed possible.

"Pick-up-your-damn-feet-and-move-to-that-ball-what-do-you-need-an-invitation?" Coach hollered.

. . . *thump . . . thump . . . thump . . .*

The ground strokes hypnotized me.

Trent moved me from one side of the court to the other and back again, forcing me to hit expert shots while running at top speed.

"Look alive, look alive . . ."

. . . *thump . . .*

"Rotate your hips toward the net; it's going to go out, going out . . ."

. . . *thud . . .*

"Out! Told you. You've got the open court. Take advantage. Rotate your hips when you hit a crosscourt shot, or the shot is playing you."

. . . *thump . . .*

"Rotate!" he screamed.

. . . *thump . . . thunk.* The ball crashed into his tennis shoe. He tripped slightly as he tried getting out of the line of fire. I laughed.

43

"Was that rotated enough?" I asked innocently.

"Smart mouth."

"Admit it, Coach, you like the precision."

"Yeah, show-off."

"You *love* the precision, Coach."

"Love it," he mocked. "Do it again."

. . . *thump* . . .

"Can she do it? Does she have the skill?" He jogged across the court, trying to break my concentration. "Batter, batter, batter, swing!"

Keeping one eye on the moving target, one on the ball, I set up the shot.

. . . *thump* . . . *thunk.* Amazingly it hit the side of his shoe.

"Dead-on-target, Coach."

"Shit," he said, gently shaking his head.

"What was that?"

"Shoot," he said, clarifying.

"I'm telling Annie you're corrupting me with bad language. She won't be happy." Annie is Coach's wife.

"Tattletales will not be tolerated. Are you through jabbering?"

"Yes."

"Can I hit a ball now? Can practice continue?"

"Sure, Coach."

Thump . . . thump . . . thump . . . Penn balls flew skillfully, precisely, obscenely inside the lines.

Suddenly remembering Luke, I glanced toward the bleachers—he was still there, waiting, watching. I waved. He waved back. I hoped he wasn't bored out of his mind. But it didn't matter either way. That was the thing about tennis: it took all my focus. Who watched didn't matter. Couldn't matter. I was a circus animal, trained to perform.

The ball sailed toward me.

I took command straightaway and hit a deep angle. Coach ran far right to meet it. His return was marginal. With him out of position, the court opened. The court lines framed my shot; I saw exactly where to place the ball. I hit it clean. It cleared the net easily. Streamlined. The yellow ball fell with vengeance right where I knew it would. Trent struggled, bending, running to the opposite side of the open court. "Agg! Uh, uh." He barely got a racquet on it.

Again, the court opened.

I had the easy put-away—a scorching forehand on the unmanned half. Coach saw no use trying to run it down. The point was mine. Coach looked at me for two, maybe three seconds. Wanted to commend me, but stopped short. After all, I was only doing my job. But his smirk said it all: he respected the shot. He'd taught me how: hit the angle, open the court, the point is mine.

Trent's new employee appeared, shuddering as Trent bellowed commands. Trent was a difficult boss: he went through workers at an alarming rate—so much so that I didn't bother learning their names. This particular helper guy was hesitant and terrorized, prompting me to brand him Skittish Helper Guy. Between points, he monitored his watch, waiting for the magic number that would cause his freedom.

"Move, move, move!" Trent screamed. "Chip and charge . . . chip and charge." Emotionless, I obeyed.

Thump . . . thump . . . thump . . .

"Keep that attitude in line," Coach lectured. "Don't roll your eyes at me! Hustle! Focus, now. Hit it like you mean it."

. . . thump . . .

Trent pointed at Skittish Helper Guy, demanding that he take over as my drill partner. Skittish Helper Guy flicked graceful lobs into the sky for me to slam into whichever box of the court Coach screamed.

"Right!" *. . . thump . . .*

"Left!" *. . . thump . . .*

"Right! Snap your wrist!" *. . . thump . . .*

"Right!" *. . . thump . . .*

When an opponent hits a nice arch-filled lob, the

46

point can be won by hitting an overhead shot. I missed a few easy overheads at my last tournament. Unacceptable. Now Coach filled my drills with overheads, rubbing it in, making me ashamed. I'll never miss another one, trust me.

"Remember, an overhead is all about the wrist snap."

"I know."

"Get some control here, Braxton. Slam the ball—look alive, woman, slam that ball! Get some air under your feet. Jump, Braxton! Snap! Remember placement. *Feel the point, feel the point* . . ."

"Left!" . . . *thump* . . .

"Left!"

I struggled. "Agg!" . . . *thump* . . .

"Good girl."

Skittish Helper Guy stopped to gather the balls that littered the court like flecks of gold. This was my cue to take a breather. I walked to Luke, panting and sucking down water. Sweat trickled down the back of my neck, cooling small portions of my skin.

"You hit the ball so hard," he said.

"Force and placement are the key ingredients."

"Oh."

I sat next to him. "I changed to this racquet a few months ago. It's got a bigger sweet spot. I'm still getting used to it."

"Sweet spot?" he asked.

"Yeah, it's this." I laid my hand on the strings in the middle of the racquet. "You don't have control unless you hit it here."

"You call it sweet?"

"Everybody does. That's what it is—a sweet spot."

"For real?"

"I promise. I'm not making it up." I was talking to a Greek god whose entire face was one big sweet spot. I *knew* about sweet spots.

"This is fun for you?" he asked.

"Yes."

I gulped water. Luke drank most of my Diet Coke. A pattern of his teeth marks covered the paper rim.

"I usually practice earlier, but Coach had a meeting. It's nice to have an audience." I had no idea what to say, so I kept stating the obvious.

We sat in silence, Luke and I: the Greek God and the sweaty girl with the dirty T-shirt. With his feet resting on the bottom bleacher, he strummed my racquet as if it was a guitar. Abruptly he stopped, cocked his head my way, stared at my nose, and finally gazed back across the empty court. I happen to have a well-shaped nose, so it didn't rattle me.

I couldn't think of a thing to say. I knew what to do with a tennis ball—slam the sucker across the court. But

Luke Kimberlin wasn't a tennis ball. Tennis balls were afraid of me. Luke clearly wasn't. His confidence felt dangerous: the way he drank my Diet Coke, the way he sat watching me, unafraid of Coach's bellows. I liked his attitude. I wished it was mine.

"We can go for a swim after, if you want," he said.

"Oh . . . I can't, my ride will be here."

"My sister could give you a ride home."

I glanced at my watch. "It's too late; my mom's already left by now. Thanks anyway . . . Luke." I said his name aloud just to hear myself say it.

"What?"

"Huh?"

"Did you say something?"

"No."

"Oh."

Skittish Helper Guy dragged two sparkly ball machines onto the court. Trent followed, mumbling gruffly.

"Bringing out the big guns now. You're gonna love this. I love this," I said.

Coach scratched his shaved scalp and glanced around the court until I came into view. "Your father isn't paying me big bucks to watch you sit around with your friends. Get your lazy butt over here or I'll make you run sprints!"

"He's kind of bossy," I explained.

Luke shrugged. "I gotta go anyway, Holloway. Bruce will be waiting at the pool. I'll see you later, OK?"

I said something terrifically stupid, like, "You will?"

"Hall!" Coach bellowed.

"Later," Luke said.

I could only smile as I returned to the baseline.

"Why are you limping?" Trent said. "Blisters?"

"My toe. Caught the corner of a chair before practice. Wasn't wearing shoes. Smashed it right in. It aches," I said, trying to catch a glimpse of Luke through the windscreen.

"An ache doesn't cause a limp."

"Was an ache at first, now it's more like a pain."

"Which toe?"

"Right foot. Second toe." I kicked off my shoe. Luke had vanished completely.

Coach knelt, eyes widened as I removed my bloody sock. He gingerly prodded my naked second toe. "Braxton, it's swollen like a balloon. It's purple!"

"That's what I'm saying. I'll ice it when I get home."

"Ice?" he said, disbelieving. He ran his finger over it, his touch full of fear. It was a toe, not a bomb. I'd never seen him like this. Maybe he'd been in the sun too long and was delirious from the heat.

I removed my toe from his gentle grasp. "I'll ice it."

"Can you walk?"

"Walk? Hello? Been running after tennis balls for half an hour, Coach."

"Could be broken." My six-foot-three, 220-pound tennis coach looked to the heavens for help. *"Broken,"* he said, gasping.

"It's not broken. I swear."

"The Cherry Creek Invitational is coming up. You'll be a sitting duck!"

"It's not broken." Why all the fuss? I played injured all the time. Once when my elbow was the size of a grapefruit, even.

"Wiggle it," he screamed.

I wiggled. It wiggled fine.

"It's not broken," I said for the third time

• Chapter Five •

Holding my bloody sock in one hand and my sweaty shoe in the other, I hobbled to a poolside table, squinting in the hazy afternoon sun. Compassion got the best of Trent; he cut practice short and bought us glasses of iced tea. He sat with me while I waited for my ride home.

"We'll practice an extra hour tomorrow. What a hassle. Braxton, next time put some shoes on or watch where you're going. Trying to give a man a heart attack or what?"

"It'll be fine."

"I talked to Janie yesterday," Trent said softly, changing the subject from the pain of my toe to the pain of Janie's mind.

My heart sort of sank. "How's she doing?"

"She's getting better. I don't think she'll be coming home right away. They're trying to find the right medication for her."

"Oh," I said.

In addition to being my doubles partner, Janie was my fiercest competition and the only close friend I'd made in all my years on the junior tennis circuit. Trent used to be her coach, too.

She'd trained with Trent for eight months. Eight months of fun, as far as I was concerned. Janie was a goofball, an expert at cracking dumb jokes. She lived, breathed, and slept tennis. On court her apt skills kept me hustling. But tennis aside, the girl hated, and I mean *hated*, her dad.

There are two kinds of tennis parents: the kind I have, encouraging but semi-removed (until lately, that is), and the kind Janie Alessandro had, demanding and mean. Janie Alessandro's father was the scariest tennis parent I've ever seen, and I've seen them all. He screamed constantly. Red-faced. Vein at his temple surging. Ugly eyes bulging. He shouted insults at Janie for minor tennis infractions. It was humiliating.

Trent banned him from practices, claiming Janie's father was "detrimental to her ability to succeed." He couldn't ban him from tournaments, though. No father, after spending all that cash, *skips* the tournaments.

"Know what I hate about tennis?" Janie would ask, her voice like a songbird's.

"What?"

"My dad."

"Understandable."

Her brow would crinkle. "My brain is gonna explode. I think I'm getting an ulcer."

"Hang in there," I'd say. "It'll be OK."

She'd be eased, her tension softened. "Know what I *like* about tennis?"

"What?"

"I've got the strokes," she'd say. "I especially like it that one day I'm going to be ranked higher than you—"

"Not likely."

"—be better than you, leave your butt in the dust."

"Yeah, right. I'm ranked number four, Janie darling. Four! You're what, seventeenth now?"

"Seventh, excuse you. And quickly rising."

"Wow, I'm scared."

"You will be."

The USTA National Open Girls 14's in Utah last month was where it all went down. Neither Janie's parents nor mine could make the trip, so Trent and his wife,

Annie, drove us. I'd just won my semifinal match and settled into the stands, Trent on one side of me, Annie on the other, to watch Janie grind out her semifinal. Her opponent, Caitlin Stark, was a wily player, but Janie had won their last match.

I always rooted for Janie, but more so that day because if she prevailed, we'd face each other in the final. I couldn't think of anyone I'd rather battle for a trophy.

And then I saw him, Janie Alessandro's father, standing courtside like a stalker, watching Janie serve.

"Oh no," I'd said, pointing. "Coach, look!"

Just then the lineswoman made a bad call in Caitlin's favor. Janie's maniac father leapt onto the court and threatened to *slap* the lineswoman. All hell broke loose, as one could expect. Out of nowhere, Caitlin's parents and outraged spectators rushed the court as well, yelling and shoving. The umpire was frantic.

Trent said something like, "Now he's done it, the bastard." Tournament security started arresting people. Standing in the middle of the chaos, Janie somehow got punched in the jaw. No one to this day knows who did it.

When the melee settled, Janie was found passed out cold on the service line, her hand still expertly gripping her racquet. Trent had to carry her off the court. When she finally came to, she wasn't Janie Alessandro anymore. Tennis pressure had turned her into a basket case. Babbling incoherently, she was unable to make eye contact with Trent, or anyone else. She lost her edge, I guess, along with her mind.

She's housed in a "special care" hospital called Wellsprings Mental Health Facility—a loony bin. Janie Alessandro is now a cautionary tale to tennis parents everywhere.

It's happened before—fierce, talented girls dropping off the circuit suddenly, never to be heard from again. I always figured they were flawed in some way. Weak. But I knew Janie; heck, that girl could *play*. If it could happen to Janie Alessandro, it could happen to anyone.

It could happen to me.

I didn't want to go to practice after the Janie fiasco, but Coach made me—said I should take out my frustrations on court, that it would help. It hadn't yet. But I didn't want to tell him that, because then he'd keep talking about her even more than he already did. The only way I knew how to deal with what happened to Janie was to *not* think about her. But I was struggling; lately, Polly's similar personality kept Janie on my mind.

"Janie asked about you. She's curious to know why you haven't gone to see her. Why haven't you?"

My voice wobbled. "I don't know."

That was a lie. I did know. What happened to her scared the crap out of me, and *I didn't want to see her.*

Oddly, I didn't think about Janie when I was on court. It came in small slices, usually when I was alone: the throaty cackle of her laugh, or the baby-blue shoestrings on her tennis shoes, or the image of her pained face dropping to that Utah court popped into my head.

"But you said you were going to. I told your mother we had it all worked out," Coach said.

I shrugged.

Coach sighed. "Janie doesn't have the mental toughness for the game, Hall," he said. "She didn't do anything wrong; she just doesn't have the head for it."

Coach had tried convincing me of it before. But it was a lie. That girl *was* tennis. Tennis balls *worshiped* her. "I know," I said, hoping we could stop talking about it.

"Janie isn't like you, Hall. You have the talent *and* the head. You're tough. She isn't."

I shrank in my seat. That killed me—Coach disrespecting her like that. Plus, it wasn't true, about my toughness. He didn't know I was fighting to find his once omnipresent voice; he didn't know I needed that voice to win. Lately, I felt I was *this close* to becoming Janie.

Coach stopped talking for a while. I moved my chair, getting the sun out of my eyes. We'd solved nothing here concerning Janie. He knew it and so did I.

"And another thing," Coach said, as if suddenly remembering. "I don't want you bringing people to practice, either. You're here to work, not to show off for a bunch of boys."

"Show off?"

"I'm not asking. I'm telling."

"Are you mad at me, Coach?"

"Tennis is an *individual* sport. And I—"

"He's the finest boy I've ever seen. Except for Roger Federer."

"Hmpf." Coach's body remained calm, hands relaxed on the table, but his eyes were stricken by my remark. Nostrils flared. A general look of *Oh my God* settled into his features. As in *Oh my God—she's discovered boys.*

This shift happened before my eyes. I was no longer a person to Trent, but a *player.* A valuable prodigy that needed every bone unbroken. Every spare ounce of energy needed to be devoted to hitting a ball over a net, not to *boys.* Boys were worse than broken toes.

But nothing was worse than Janie Alessandro's broken mind. Coach said nothing more. It was the *way* he said nothing more that bothered me. I felt I should apologize. But I was afraid to see Janie, and how could I truly be sorry for liking the Greek God?

• Chapter Six •

The doors slid open, welcoming us. They know us here, my mom and me, by name. Employees at Tennis Emporium get a commission on each sale, and for a long time now our salesman, Wesley, who looks like a Ken doll, has had dibs on the commission we generate. We purchase a lot. The commission is high. Wesley loves us. The strain on my mom's face prompts him to give us a straight ten percent discount every time. My mother says he's a "nice boy."

"Did you remember the list?" my mom asked.

I dug it from my pocket. "I could use some new underwear."

"Let's concentrate on tennis gear. I don't have time to be running all over town."

"I wear underwear when I play tennis. I suppose I don't *have* to, though. Course, if it's breezy and my tennis skirt flies up, it could be quite a spectacle, could be—"

"Fine, we'll stop at Target on the way home. You're full of sass for a girl who didn't empty the dishwasher this morning."

"Not my turn. Brad's turn."

"That's what he said about you."

"Ladies, ladies, hello."

"Hi, Wes."

"Hello, Wesley," my mom said. "Shoes first?"

"Sure thing."

I walked ahead.

"Have you heard anything about Janie? How's she doing?" Wes called from behind me.

I felt my mom's eyes on the back of my head, hot, burning. I looked straight ahead, pretending I hadn't heard, and stopped at a shoe bench.

"Wesley," my mom said, "Hall doesn't really want to discuss it. She and her tennis coach are dealing with it."

Way to go, Mom! I caught her eye. She winked. I exhaled. Answering to Coach about it was one thing; having to answer to Wes wasn't necessary.

"Oh, OK. No problem," Wes said, having realized his blunder. "Shoes, then . . ."

He grabbed a pair, lacing them as I took a seat.

"What size is that?" I asked.

"Your size."

"I'll need a half size bigger. My toes feel too tight in the ones I've been wearing."

Selecting a different shoe, he laced again. I slid my foot in, making noises so everyone would laugh.

"Ahh . . . Wilson DST 02, women's size eight. Pure bliss, ladies and gentlemen. Pure bliss."

"Room enough?"

"Perfect."

Wes looked to my mom. "Mrs. Braxton?" He referred to her, always, for the quantity because she possessed the credit card.

"Three pair."

"I only need two," I said.

Sweaty shoes cause blisters, to which I'm prone. Alternating shoes is important so sweat-soaked shoes have a chance to dry before they're worn again (gross, I know). I don't need three pair. I can make do with two.

"We'll get three."

"But I only need—"

"Three," she said to Wes. He headed to the stockroom.

Perfect example of the weird stuff that's been happening. *Three pair!* I used to have to beg for *one* new pair, and now she's ponying up for three pair of Wilson

DST 02s at ninety-five dollars a pop, willingly. We argue over *underwear,* but suddenly tennis gear is a necessity, like oxygen or water. It's unsettling.

Tennis is a hugely expensive sport. Coaches, shoes, tournament entry fees—it adds up. Some out-of-state tournaments require plane tickets *and* hotel stays. Heck, even the gas to get me to the country club my own family can't afford to join costs an easy thousand a year! We scrimp and save any way we can. We never buy three pair!

"What's next?" my mom asked.

"Racquets," I said.

"Wesley will catch up."

Prince. Best stick ever. Great for my game. Two hundred bucks apiece, unstrung. Coach will string them for me later. He likes to do it himself, wants it done right. I grabbed two. This isn't negotiable. Have to have racquets. This racquet. Others mess up my game.

As I searched for my racquets my mom moved down the aisle to study rows of thick sport socks.

Wes caught up to me, balancing shoe boxes. "New racquets? I thought you were getting free Prince racquets."

I shook my head, indicating my mom's ignorance of the matter. We stepped aside. "I am. But I left my club locker unlocked and my bag got hauled off to the lost and found. My racquets weren't in it when I got it back.

63

My fault, really. And I'm not due another shipment of Prince racquets for a month. I thought I had a spare in my room, but turns out that was the one that sort of broke a few weeks ago," I said.

"Broke? How?" he asked. Wes enjoyed scandals.

"It sort of got slammed into the court after a lousy point. I sort of slammed it."

Wes made an O with his mouth. "I see."

"For racquet abuse, Coach made me do laps around the court while singing the theme song from *Rocky*. You believe that?"

"That was harsh of him."

"No kidding."

My mom rejoined us, holding five pair of Thorlo socks. Eleven bucks a pair. "Are we done?"

"I need more blister crap."

"Don't say 'crap.' "

"Blister stuff."

I gathered Blister Band-Aids, Dr. Scholl's Molefoam, Coban tape, and extra Coban tape since I lose it constantly.

"I'm done."

"Step right to the register, ladies. I'll get you squared away."

I prepared myself for the strained look on my mom's

face as she handed Wesley her credit card. Never enough money, everything so expensive. A good stick costs two hundred dollars. It's no one's fault. She knows this. I know this. My talent requires equipment; the equipment costs money. So I braced myself for the strain, except this time it wasn't there. A hint of something else rested on her face . . . it was hope, I think. I'm pretty sure it was hope.

• Chapter Seven •

I walked down the street, finding Polly loitering on the barren curb in front of Eve's house. She drank what looked like lemonade out of a clear plastic pitcher. Her lips were bright orange with lip gloss. It made me want to laugh. "What are you sitting out here for? Eve gone?"

She motioned to the opened garage door. "You'll see."

I ambled up the driveway just as Eve came out of the garage. "Hey," she said. "I just tried to call you. My mom and I are going to the Castle Rock outlet mall. So I can't hang out. Sorry."

Her mom stepped out of the house, digging through her purse, getting into their car. Eve glanced back, knowing she had to go.

Now was as good a time as any. I pulled out the crumpled, cola-stained cup from my pocket and held it up. "Guess what this is."

Eve shrugged impatiently. "A piece of trash?"

"Luke Kimberlin," I proclaimed, "drank from this cup! *My* cup. He watched me practice at the club!"

That got her attention. "Really? Cool. Has he called you?"

"Well, no. Should he have?"

"When are you gonna see him again?" she asked, wanting something solid.

"Maybe at the club."

"When is that gonna be?" she pressed.

I expected celebration, not an interrogation. "Eve, you don't get it—Luke talked to me *on purpose*. It's a big deal."

Brake lights pulsed red as Eve's mom backed out. We stepped to the grass. Polly hadn't moved from the curb. Eve's eyes darted toward the car, preoccupied.

"But you don't know if he likes you. He only watched you play tennis. That doesn't mean—"

"Eve—"

Her mom beeped the horn. Eve edged away. "I gotta go. We're meeting my aunt up there. It's an hour drive. Tell me about Luke later, OK?"

"Sure," I said, feeling drowned.

As Eve drove away, Polly walked over, orange lips blazing. "Told you," she said. "Want some lemonade?"

I handed her my used Diet Coke cup. "Guess what this is," I said.

With no other shade in sight, we trudged across the blacktop of the nearby grade school, our steps clumsy in the swelling afternoon heat. The playground was deserted save for a few boys riding bikes in the dirt. We situated ourselves under the shade of an awning. Polly was genuinely interested, and I was grateful.

"Luke Kimberlin!" she said, riled up. "I can't believe you didn't tell me before. Luke Kimberlin . . . wow . . . this is exactly what you wanted!"

I know it was silly, but hearing his name made me happy. I shook myself out of my own little world and glanced at my watch. "Hey, Polly, aren't you supposed to be at math camp today? Like right now?"

She smacked her orange lips defiantly. "I'm supposed to be a genius, too, and I'm not that, either."

"You ditched?" I asked, astonished.

"Math camp blows."

"I bet."

"Sucks to have math homework in June. Besides, it's not like I'm stupid. But A's aren't good enough, I've got to get A-pluses. Maren wants me to be a chemist like her. I can't do that being average. I've got to be exceptional. Do I look like I want to be a chemist?" she asked, hugging the nearly empty plastic pitcher.

"No."

She sighed. "I've been to work with Maren. It sucked."

I felt the need to hug her or something, but she didn't look like she wanted a hug. Looked more like she wanted to punch someone.

"But you're good at math?" I asked.

"Duh."

"You don't like being smarter than everyone else?"

"Whose side are you on, anyway?"

"Yours."

"How many hours a day do you spend playing tennis?"

"Five. Three hours with Coach. A couple hours on my own, practicing serves."

"Five," she said smugly. "Including math camp, I spend four hours a day doing math problems."

I shrugged. "What's your point?"

"We're twins. We're slaves to sports and numbers."

"Yeah, I guess," I said uneasily.

"So be on my side. I don't want to be a chemist. I hate math."

Before I knew Polly, I thought she was nerdy. Back in April the seventh grade held their annual science fair. Most of the projects looked like they'd been thrown together the night before. Battery demonstrations, erupting volcanoes, and models of the solar system packed the room.

Polly's was different. She performed an experiment charting the growth rate of bacteria at different temperatures. Her booth contained petri dishes, a microscope, and an array of drawings of bacteria. Teachers hovered over her like she was the next Jonas Salk.

At the end of the day the principal announced that even though "learning was its own reward," he had plaques for the best projects.

When Polly's name was called, she hauled ass to the front of the room and collected her grand prize, her face beet red from embarrassment. Her mom cheered loudly; it was clear she took the achievement personally. Talk about embarrassing. The more I knew about Polly, the more I appreciated my mom's lack of involvement.

Polly's mother seemed to be an exact replica of Janie's bewildering father. I'd go mad if I had parents like that. My mom asking about Janie was bad enough.

I was lost in my thoughts when Polly pointed her bony finger in my face. "Are you gonna let Luke Kimberlin stick his tongue in your mouth?"

"Funny, Polly," I wryly said. "Do you think he should've called by now?"

"Don't know," she said.

"I'm not a country club girl. I wonder why he likes me, if he does."

She elbowed my arm. "Why wouldn't he? You're likable."

We sat for a few seconds.

"So, are you?" she asked.

"Am I what?"

"Luke's tongue."

"Heck, yeah," I said.

Polly laughed hysterically.

The air was cooler than usual. I'd forgotten to pack a warm-up jacket in my tennis bag, so I froze in my T-shirt, bouncing up and down on court, trying to get warm. I corralled the balls out of my way so I wouldn't trip. Checked my watch—I'd only been here an hour. Still had an hour to try to wrestle Coach's voice back into me.

Rise, Coach, rise. Please.

Step to the baseline. Bounce ball. Separate hands.

Racquet back. Extend racquet. Make contact. Follow through. Out. By a fourth of an inch. Barely out. Hmmm.

Breathe. In and out. Keep warm. Ignore the breeze. Ignore chattering teeth. The ball matters. A fourth of an inch matters. Let everything else fall away. Let Trent's voice rise.

Rise, Coach, rise.

Bounce ball. Separate hands. Racquet back—

"Hey, Hall!"

I whipped my head around. Polly was crouched down, looking at me through a patch of the torn windscreen. Thank God I wasn't hallucinating now, too. "What are you doing?"

"Came to watch you practice. How do I get in?"

I pointed. "You gotta go through that hole." I jogged over and held back the jagged wire fence. "Careful, it'll rip your shirt."

"Whew," she said, standing upright again, holding a paper bag, dismayed. "*This* is where you practice? Yuk."

"How did you know where to find me?"

"Melissa told me. I want to watch you play. So here I am."

"What's in that bag?"

She bit her lip. Scrunched up her nose. "You'll find out in a minute, nosy." She looked back. "Melissa?"

72

"How do I get in?" Melissa wailed.

"Melissa is here, too?" I said, astonished.

"Sure, why not? I wanted Eve to come, but she said she had something else to do."

Melissa struggled, getting in. "Hey, Hall," she said.

"Are those weeds growing out of the court?" Polly asked.

"Yeah, this court . . . sucks. I usually practice alone, you know, so I can concentrate." I felt my face burn. I was thrown. Aside from Melissa's occasional questions, my friends and my tennis never mixed. Eve would never . . . I laughed at the sight of them, my two separate worlds blending like this.

Polly freed a homemade sign from the paper bag and began hitching it to the metal court fence. Melissa dropped her jacket and helped. I stood back, watching, revived.

Melissa tipped it this way and that, getting it right, while Polly joined me, slugging my arm. "Look," she said. "You're in a parade. This tennis court is your float. Wave to the nice children!" She pretended she was a float queen and began waving to imaginary people.

The sign read GO, HALL!

Not wanting to be left out, Melissa waved, too, to no one.

I studied the sign. Plastic pink flowers were glued onto it, around the lettering. It wasn't haphazard; that sign took planning. "Who did those flowers?"

"Me," Polly said. "I'm artsy. Just because I've got a brain for numbers doesn't mean I'm not artsy."

Polly seemed able to stir herself easily into any situation—Eve's house, my tennis life—yet at the same time she seemed to belong nowhere and to nothing. The girl boggled my mind. She reminded me so much of Janie. Though I felt terrible when Coach or my mom tried talking to me about Janie, I was fine with Polly's resemblance to her—remembering the fun Janie and I had before she lost her mind.

Despite the cold my face continued burning. I was embarrassed, delighted. "How come you did this?"

Polly slung her arm around me in her eager way. "Because you don't hate tennis, right? So here we are. Play."

"I can't play, I don't have an opponent; I just come here to serve."

"So serve. We don't mind, right, Melissa?"

"No, we don't care," Melissa said.

They aligned themselves against the fence. Waiting.

Bounce, bounce, bounce. Separate hands. Racquet back. Toss the ball—

"Should I cheer yet?" Polly blurted out.

The ball fell limply to the court. My concentration faltered. What concentration? It was gone. "You don't cheer in tennis. You clap politely for a good shot. You say nothing during a serve."

"Yeah," Melissa said, as if she knew.

"Oh," Polly said, uninterested in those confining regulations. "Maybe I could find a place to cheer if you would hurry up and serve."

Enough of this. I stuffed my pockets with Penn balls for easy access and shot them at her and Melissa, one, two, three, four . . .

"Hey! Quit! No fair!" Polly squealed.

Grabbing the flimsy paper sack, she spread it across them, as if it offered protection. Ha!

Five, six, seven, eight more balls . . .

"Where's my cheering?" I asked, laughing so hard my gut ached. "I don't hear any cheering! These are excellent shots. Go ahead and cheer. I'm waiting."

"Agg!" Polly said, laughing too.

• Chapter Eight •

Piles of tennis academy brochures are infiltrating my world with no letup in sight. Thick, glossy brochures, pamphlets, and catalogs from every warm state in America are basically *breeding* in my parents' mailbox. I can barely keep up with them.

The postman has a streak of wickedness. When I politely asked him to stop delivering the brochures—to simply chuck them in the trash—he sighed at me, mumbled something about a "federal offense," and then unmercifully shoved a bunch more into the box, out of spite, probably.

I've managed to intercept a few thick packets. Unfortunately, one from Bickford Academy in Florida slipped by me and is now in the clutches of my parents. The brochures I've taken—from California and Florida—are loaded with bright pictures of teens gripping racquets and holding trophies. The captions say things like "Make a Winner for a Lifetime" and "Our Teaching Pros Make the Difference."

They don't fool me. I know the statistics. Only three or four elite kids out of the two hundred kids from an academy will have a chance to make it on the professional circuit. Those aren't good odds. Even the exceptionally gifted won't become top-ten players as professionals. They'll be ranked in the fifties or sixties for their entire careers. A champion—what a joke.

Recently, my parents have been going over the stack of brochures that managed to get through. A few times a week they sit at the kitchen table and discuss them. Often now, my face has the imprint of the heating vent on it as I eavesdrop, listening to them talk *about* me in *regard* to tennis.

Mom: "They're *children,* Frank."

Dad: "They're playing sports in the fresh air."

Mom: "It's a boot camp."

Dad: "They have to have rules. Would you rather have a hundred kids running amok, doing as they pleased?"

Mom: "Their childhoods are consumed by rankings and tournament titles. It's not healthy, Frank. It's not normal."

Dad: "Normal is watching five hours of TV a day. Normalcy breeds mediocrity."

Mom: "Running for president with that slogan?"

Dad: "This guy today—he might be exactly what Hall needs. Vivian, with this extra money we've got now—"

Mom: "We can't use all that money on Hall. What about the boys? What about college funds? It's not fair to—"

Dad: "We could—"

Mom: "We can't send her to an academy for a single year, then make her come home. If we make the commitment, it's got to be for the duration."

Dad: "I know, I know . . ."

I didn't know what guy they were talking about, but regardless, my mom is definitely the Weak Link. When she says things like "They're *children,* Frank" and "It's a boot camp," I feel she's on my side. And I plan to play off her doubts as much as I'm able.

Lately they've acquired calculators and have been adding up mortgage payments, food, and car expenses. Then they subtract bits of money from specific columns, hoping an extra four thousand dollars a month for tennis academy tuition will emerge.

They're acting like insane accountants now because my grandpa is dead. He died three years ago, but his house in Chicago recently sold. They got a big check last week. My parents want to use my dead grandpa's money to help banish me to a tennis academy. They refer to this money as the Dead Grandpa Bonus Fund. My grandpa Floyd was a chef, not a sports fan.

"Ready, Hall?" my mom called.

"Yeah, just a sec."

"Hurry up, we're already late."

I grabbed my Prince stick. My mom had the engine running by the time I reached the garage. Her lips were glazed with lipstick, her good lipstick, the kind reserved for dinner reservations and anniversaries. Looked like she was going someplace special. My dad was perched in the front seat as if on his way to a celebration. The jig was up.

"How come you're both driving me?"

"We thought we'd watch you practice," my dad said.

Most of the time I felt lucky to get a ride at all. The club was clear across town on Broadmoor Valley Road, a forty-minute drive to and fro. They never watched my lessons, not even when I was eight. "Both of you? Both of you are watching me practice?"

"Sure," my dad said. "It's a splendid day, why not?"

A splendid day? I would have jumped out of the car right then, but we were already a block from home and traveling at roughly thirty-five miles per hour. Words like "splendid" weren't part of my dad's vocabulary.

My parents weren't club members—they needed guest passes or they'd be tossed out. Since technically I wasn't a member, either, I couldn't provide passes.

"Can't get in without a pass," I told them, gloating.

"Trent gave us passes," my mom said.

"Gave you . . . Why did he do that?"

My mom turned in her seat, glaring. "Well, excuse us for taking an interest in your life."

An interest, ha! We drove in silence the rest of the way.

The air roasted me from the inside out. It was Africa hot. Heat swelled from the sky and ground at equal intensities; the fiery court surface threatened to swallow my legs in flames. My parents and I fell through the gate of court 3. Trent bounded over. Trent never *bounds*.

"Glad you could make it," he said, using an elegant tone of voice. "Hot one today. Can I get you something to drink? Snack bar is just over yonder."

"No, we're fine. Thanks," my mom said.

"Been a while," my dad said. "Please tell me you're

bald by choice and not from the stress of coaching the enigma."

Coach chuckled. "No. Wouldn't put it past her, though. Girl keeps me on my toes."

Something was askew. Trent was famous for his dislike of tennis parents. Normally he didn't even like encouraging but semi-removed parents like mine (until lately, that is), and here he was bounding over to greet them, being polite. Cracking jokes, no less.

As my parents moseyed to the bleachers, Trent grabbed my arm. "Face north," he said, "and play hard."

"But, Coach, I—"

"Face north. Play hard."

Coach knows I prefer facing south on court 3. Facing south, I can view sailboats that drift in the lake. Occasionally they mesmerize me and I get clobbered by a ball. Trent sighs like I've committed a huge sin, then makes me face north, so my view is the club's ugly brown fitness center building. Says if I keep goofing off in practice he's gonna make me hit on condemned court 15, which doesn't even have a net, and *then* I'll be sorry.

"Did you hear me, Hall? North."

"I heard you. I'm going. Jeez."

"Hall." Coach looked at me, jaw set, nostrils flared,

brown eyes fierce. Urgency stabbed his words. "Play hard."

I nodded and shut up.

Skittish Helper Guy materialized on the court and practice began. Trent joined my parents at the set of small bleachers—the very same bleachers that Luke Kimberlin, the Greek God, had occupied two weeks prior.

... *thump* ... *thump* ... *thump* ...

"Hustle, hustle . . . hit a passing shot, go, go!"

... *thump* ...

"Nice! Do it again."

It was only when I couldn't find Trent's voice that fear set in. Now, with Trent screaming at me, all was well again. Immediately I was in the zone. It's a place where everything is blank: crowds, umpires, opponents—they don't exist. I see only the fuzzy yellow Penn ball. Flying.

The ball is mine. I own it. Dominate it. It travels to me, it's mine. I slam it, punish it. Threaten it, throttle it. Smacking it as hard as I can ... *thump* ... Goes where I tell it to go. Obeys me. Eager to please. See only the ball, nothing else. Hear the twang I cherish. My head is wonderfully blank. Perfection rests in my blank head. It's beautiful. I'm beautiful. It's only after I win a point that I realize I'm playing at all. It's automatic and it's the sweetest thing ever, the zone.

When a Penn ball hits the racquet, my fingers feel it first. My grip tightens slightly at impact. Pressure enters my wrist, travels into my shoulder, and vibrates through the rest of my body. I hit each ball with every cell of my body. In the zone I don't have to try, it just happens. On impact I exhale, shudder as I hear the twang, and fill with joy.

. . . thump . . . thump . . . thump . . .

Skittish Helper Guy ran down my passing shots, heaving.

. . . thump . . .

"Placement," Coach screamed, "get it, get there . . ."

"Agg!"

. . . thump . . .

"Good. Again."

. . . thump . . . thump . . . thump . . .

I stole a glance at the bleachers. Thomas Fountain had joined Coach and my parents—he was "the guy." Coach ceased yelling. Instead, he told my "warrior story."

". . . so she's at this tournament in Vegas—the Great Pumpkin Sectional Championship. It's the semifinals of the toughest draw she's ever faced. Hall's dominating. Destroying the opposition. Going to win, no question."

"Win, definitely," my dad said.

"Out of desperation her opponent rushes the net and

tries to volley. Hall shoots from the baseline—I'm stunned she even *got* to the damn ball. Brings her racquet back, back, back, the whole court is silent, and then . . . *Boom!* Slams the ball at this girl, hard."

"Hit her with the ball," my dad clarified.

"Yeah," Trent said, "slams the ball into her and *breaks the girl's arm*!"

"It was an accident, of course," my mom said, worried. "Hall wasn't *aiming* for the girl."

"Wanted to win," Trent said. "That's the intensity of her concentration. Hall doesn't *allow* girls to hit winning volley shots. Broke her arm and *wasn't sorry.*"

"I'm sure she was sorry," my mom said.

"No, she wasn't," Trent protested. "Didn't do it on purpose, but trust me, she wasn't sorry."

"Hell," Thomas said.

"No shit," Trent said, laughing.

"Did she win the tournament?" Thomas asked.

"Aren't you listening? *Of course* she won."

"I'm sure she was sorry," my mom said again.

Trent told the story often, to whoever would listen. I was sure in a few years he'd be telling it in a way that had me killing the girl by slamming a ball into her face. Aside from being bossy and impatient, Trent was fond of violence.

The four of them spontaneously clapped at my effort at a lob, removing my focus.

"Hall, come over. Take a break," Trent called.

Skittish Helper Guy picked up velvety balls from the court. Thomas Fountain gawked at me as I approached. He was a former pro who taught tennis at a posh resort hotel, the Broadmoor. He'd watched me practice twice before, at Coach's invitation.

"Hello, Hall. Do you remember me?" Thomas said, offering his hand.

I wiped the sweat from my hand to shake his. Both Trent and my dad looked at me like I'd better be polite or I'd have hell to pay later on, so I said, "Yes, I do. Nice to see you again, Mr. Fountain."

My mom exhaled.

"She likes the battle of it. The bloodier the better," Trent informed him.

Thomas cracked a smile. "I can see that. Quite impressive out there, young lady."

"Thanks." I hate it when people call me things like "young lady." It's condescending. But he was a former pro, so I decided to let it slide. Plus, Trent would've hollered at me if I said anything.

I sucked down half of the water in my bottle and poured the rest on the top of my head. Cool water dribbled down my face and body, further soaking my sweat-sopped tennis dress. The four of them watched this and said nothing.

Back on court, Skittish Helper Guy set up the ball machines. I strained to seize the words of Trent and Thomas Fountain as they walked toward the gate, talking *about* me in *regard* to tennis.

"Haven't got much time. Wouldn't want her to miss her window," Coach said.

"Twelve would've been better, but at thirteen—"

"She's *barely* thirteen," Coach said.

"Possesses the game, anyway. Layered with the right shots. How is she on strategy?"

"Girl could be a general. Got the one intangible of tennis, the rhythm. Changes the pace ever so slightly to confuse her opponents."

Thomas nodded. Coach seemed satisfied as they stood near the gate. "Thanks a lot, Thomas. Sure appreciate it. If they could see her—"

"No problem. She's a hoot. Got the attitude, that's half of it. That's what they like out there."

"We'll talk later, then," Trent said. "You've got the home number?"

"Yep."

Thump . . . thump . . . thump . . .

A scheme to send me away was definitely in the plotting stages. It wasn't just my parents; Trent was in on it, too, involving former tennis pros, no less. My world was closing in. No one could be trusted. The Fourth of July was fast approaching—a third of the summer gone. Time was running out. I had to regain my champion status. I had to get my confidence back.

. . . *thump* . . . *thump* . . . *thump* . . .

Trent stood at the net. My parents were out of earshot. "Give me some control out there!" Coach screamed. "Get aggressive, charge at it. Focus on placement . . . show me some control. No bargaining now. *Place* the ball . . . dominate the point . . . go, go . . ."

"Agg!"

"Move, move, move! Braxton, wake up out there. What do you need, a nap? Dominate the ball . . . move, move, move!"

. . . *thump* . . .

"On the line, excellent."

. . . *thump* . . . *thump* . . . *thump* . . .

My parents did the wave from the bleachers, standing up with arms overhead, then sitting back down. Again, this stole my focus. I hit a backhand lob into the net.

"Nice try anyway, honey," my dad said from across the court, not realizing it was his fault.

"What the hell was that? Concentrate, Braxton," Trent bellowed. "One hundred more backhands for that mistake." He called to Skittish Helper Guy, "One hundred more." Helper Guy nodded.

. . . *thump* . . . *thump* . . . *thump* . . .

"You can do this in your sleep, no reason to miss even one. I don't care if there's an elephant in the middle of the court, you hit that ball. Kill that ball!"

Emotionless, I obeyed. *Thump* . . . *thump* . . . *thump* . . .

"In the corner, excellent."

. . . *thump* . . . *thump* . . . *thump* . . .

"On the line, good girl."

. . . *thump* . . . *thump* . . . *thump* . . .

• Chapter Nine •

As I walked in the door, Michael turned and grunted. It was his way of getting my attention. "Two of your stupid little friends left messages for you." This kind of disrespect was the main reason my friends never hung out at my house. Brad blocked my way, pretending to be the hero of a martial arts film.

"Move, Brad."

"Hi-yaaa!"

"Quit."

He flung his foot an inch from my face. "Hi-yaaa!"

"Stop it, Brad."

"I could do damage. Two hits and you'd be a dead woman."

Lately my brothers and their friends have ditched

their usual football games in favor of tae kwon do. Instead of being tackled on my way up the stairs, I'm now the endless recipient of exotically named kicks to my body and aggressive blows to my throat. They never make actual bodily contact but act like I'm lucky they spare my life on a daily basis.

"Let me by, Brad, you brat."

"Hi-yaaa!"

"I'm telling!"

"Crybaby," he said, moving aside.

I grabbed the messages. One from Eve: *Do you want to spend the night? Call me back if you do.*

And one from Polly: *Maren is going out with her boyfriend tonight. Do you want to spend the night?*

I grabbed Polly's message. *Polly's.* Not Eve's. It took no thought. Chose Polly over Eve. Snap. Like that. Surprised myself, but did it anyway. Eve would never know.

I dialed her number. "Hey, Polly. Yes, I'll be there."

Polly instructed me to walk in without knocking, but I knocked anyway. As I stood on the steps a twinge of confusion stabbed me. I considered myself a loyal person. But I was *here,* not at Eve's. And I didn't feel half as much guilt about it as I thought I should.

Polly's mom's boyfriend, a tall blond, sporting an unbuttoned shirt, greeted me. He was in his late twenties, I guessed. Since when do moms have cute boyfriends?

"I'm Pete Graham, who are you?" I followed his exposed skin upward until I reached his aqua eyes. My brothers spent their summers shirtless; somehow this was different. He snapped his fingers at me, indicating I should hand him my sleeping bag, pronto.

"I'm Holloway. Call me Hall."

"Well, that's a name, I suppose."

He was sort of a jerk. Leaning down, he grabbed my bag and stepped on a chew toy left on the floor by Sugar, the Cassinis' Labrador. As the chew toy slid violently across the floor, so did Pete, landing hard on the Mexican tile. I waited for a four-letter expletive to fly from his mouth. He didn't curse, but he *wanted* to.

"You just missed them," he said, picking himself up. "They're getting a pizza. I'll put this in Polly's room," he said, finally wrestling the sleeping bag into submission.

While he proceeded down the hallway I forged into the living room to wait. Because we all hung out at Eve's so much, this was the first time I'd been inside Polly's house. It was clean, modest. A makeshift office was set up in an alcove near the sofas. I scanned the small desk, my eyes dropping to the paper shredder beside it. It just so happened that I'd stored my confiscated tennis academy catalogs in the bottom of a bag, the very same bag that was now slung over my shoulder, which held my toothbrush and oversized sleep T-shirt.

Quickly I dropped the bag, opened it, and scraped tennis academy brochures and catalogs from its insides. I clicked on the machine. Green buttons lit the surface. Whirling, the contraption made horrific choking noises as I fed handfuls of pages into its violent jaws. *Faster, come on* . . . One, two, three down; twelve to go. They could never be traced back to me now. *Come on, dumb shredder, faster* . . .

Pete Graham entered the room carrying Diet Cokes, eyes fixed on the tower of catalogs. I sat frozen, a brochure dangling over the shredder, waiting to be yelled at, or sent to reform school, or something. His face had erased its guile. It was clear he wasn't a parent.

"Need a Coke?" he asked. "All they have is diet."

I hesitated. "Um, sure."

I'd assumed our brief conversation would be the extent of his tolerance for me, but here he was again, with beverages, no less. His attitude had changed: his indifference morphed into politeness.

"What are you doing?"

"Um, nothing . . . shredding some things."

"What are they, catalogs?"

"Something like that."

He was amused. "Something like what, catalogs?"

Something like none of his business, but he wasn't taking the hint. "Yeah, catalogs, kind of."

"Why?"

"Um . . . because."

"Well, don't let me stop you."

I shoved more in, panicked. Pete sat on one of the large sofas. He didn't try to read the pages. I wondered why the sudden courtesy.

The shredder coughed mournfully, a second from exploding. *Shut up,* I thought, *shut up, only a few more, a few more . . .*

"Hall?"

I turned innocently. "Yes?"

"I think you're supposed to take out the staples before you shred it, otherwise you get that noise."

"Oh. Thanks."

I ripped out the staples on my last booklet, for Langley Academy in California, and let the machine suck it down and shred it until it was unrecognizable.

Refreshed, I sat opposite Pete. We popped open our cans simultaneously. I wasn't sure why he waited with me. Maybe he thought he had to entertain me, or keep watch in case I put my feet on the furniture, or something.

I didn't mind. He was cute. It was like a fifty-dollar bill falling out of a birthday card from the grandma who usually sends a five.

I wondered what he thought about female athletes and the sport of tennis. I wondered if he knew tennis academies existed and that terribly misguided parents, such as my own, considered *exiling* their own children to *live at them* a grand idea.

"You're dating Polly's mom?" I stupidly asked. I have the bad habit of asking questions I know the answer to. I didn't know what else to say.

"Yep," he said. "Maren is an interesting woman."

"Oh. Uh-huh."

My mom says I've got to be careful of adults. Some of them, men especially, pretend to be nice but are actually perverts. My mom says in addition to acquiring good judgment about people and listening to my gut, I should tell her immediately if some guy, even Trent, does something that makes me uneasy. I thought maybe I shouldn't be here talking to this guy who was possibly a pervert or something. Except my gut told me Pete Graham was an OK guy so far.

Pete gauged my face for a moment, and then the mystery of his sudden respect was solved. "Holloway? Hall? You're the tennis girl, right?"

He must have realized it after he'd taken my sleeping bag. Otherwise he'd never have offered me a drink. He was neither a pervert nor polite—he was a *sports fan.* When adults discover I'm a tennis player, they become nice to me. Lately, for some reason, it makes me sad.

We were friends suddenly. "I'm talking to the famous tennis girl?" he continued. "Should I curtsy?"

"No. Only women curtsy. You could bow, though."

"So, tell me about this. How does one become a tennis star? Polly says you play at the national level?"

"I'm OK, I guess."

"Is it hard?"

"Hard? Um, certain girls are difficult to beat. The older you get, the tougher the competition."

"Does it get boring, practicing?"

His questions were misplaced. No one asked me questions like "Hard?" or "Boring?" In fact, no one talked to me about tennis; they talked *about* me in *regard* to tennis. Tennis was the dragon that needed to be slain; I was the sucker with the sword.

"It's just a game."

Pete Graham scoffed. He leaned forward, as if trying to discern if I was a fraud. "A game? What if someone's really kicking your butt? What then?"

"That's different. It's war. I'm a nation by myself and

the person on the other side of the net is a nation, too. One nation will be brought to their knees, without mercy."

"War?" he said.

"In tennis there's no second place, no ties. There are no halftimes. Coaches aren't allowed on court. Nobody's going to give you a pep talk. You're all alone. And if you aren't the winner, you're the loser. Battle to the death," I added for effect. It was true. It was *so* true in my own tennis that, again, I was briefly sad.

If you aren't the winner, you're the loser.

My answer didn't make Pete sad. It seemed to delight the heck out of him. He was like all spectators. They want suffering, agony, and distress in their athletes' victories. It's more exciting watching someone *suffer to win* than win effortlessly. If huge quantities of blood and possibly even some guts or bits of broken bones are involved, then it's *really* a quality match.

Sugar howled and ran to the door. The Cassinis were home. Polly bounced into the living room carrying a pizza. Her little brother, Teddy, dug out a piece and disappeared. Polly quickly introduced me to her mom, and before I knew it Maren and Pete Graham slipped out on their date, leaving us.

Polly's table manners were impeccable. Meticulously

cutting small pieces, she chewed each mouthful a hundred times before swallowing.

"Come on, let's finish eating in my room," she said.

Her bedroom furniture looked like it was purchased from random garage sales—a green desk, a pine headboard, a white chest of drawers. I sat at her desk, careful not to disturb her piles of math textbooks and test papers.

Her eyes deadened at the sight of them, seemingly mortified by the chunk of her life she devoted to them. "Geometry," Polly said flatly. "I'll move them." In one wide swoop of her hand, she flung the books to the floor: pages crumpled, pages tore.

"The bindings will break," I said, picking up a book.

"Leave it," Polly said.

"Yeah, but the bindings—"

"I don't care."

Polly gathered a red feather boa from her closet and slung it around her neck, transforming herself into a chorus line dancer. She applied a heavy coating of orange lip gloss, smacking her lips together to blend it. Now she was a gangster's girlfriend from the Roaring Twenties *and* a chorus line dancer. "Want to help me bury something?" she said.

"It's not a body, is it?" I asked.

She squealed. "No, don't be silly. Come along," she

urged. She grabbed a small cookie tin from her floor and led us out.

In her backyard, while Sugar sniffed around the lawn, Polly sat in the grass near a dead aspen tree and the fence, digging up the dry earth with a kitchen spoon. Her red boa flowed onto the grass.

"So, what's in the can?" I asked.

"Open it and see," she said.

"It's not a dead hamster or something, is it?" I asked. I'd once given a deceased pet hamster a shoe-box funeral in my backyard. But I was eight then.

Polly flicked out small spoonfuls of dirt, deepening the hole. Pausing, she flipped her boa out of her way, keeping its feathers from the dusty earth. Something about her face caught me—*the girl did not look human.* I pulled back like I'd touched fire.

Polly looked up suddenly. Her orange lips popped off her face. "It's not a hamster," she said. "Open it and look."

The lid came off with a *ting* sound. Inside was a balled-up red ribbon. Polly grabbed it from me and shook it so it unfolded. It read SECOND PLACE.

"I won second place at the math competition today. Out of fifty kids. We compete every so often, to shake things up," she said, rolling her eyes. She stuffed the silky ribbon back in the cookie tin and shut the lid.

Looking at me, she dropped it to its scary resting place. "Bye-bye," she said to it, waving, laughing.

She scooped dirt over it with her bare hands. Giggling. She was a kite, flying free.

Discovering Polly this summer couldn't have been a fluke. Janie had sent Polly here, somehow, to comfort me and tell me I'd be all right. Polly wasn't human— Polly was my *angel*. I mentally replaced that boa with a set of celestial wings. Yes, my angel. I didn't have to worry myself over Janie, at least not right here with Polly in the yard. Polly had risen above her talent for math. Floated right above it, with her wings. She hated it, but it hadn't broken her. And maybe, just maybe, Janie wasn't broken, either. I let myself think this. I needed to think Janie was OK.

At one o'clock in the morning Polly decided she was hungry. We creaked into the kitchen. Words echoed from the dimly lit living room.

"Polly, are you guys still up?" called Maren. "Bring in the rest of that pizza, will you?"

"And water," Pete said. "Please."

Polly grabbed bottled water. I carried the pizza.

Pete's head was propped awkwardly against a sofa pillow. Maren's blouse was on the floor, her bra on the coffee table. I sort of stood there at a loss. Surely she knew she was naked, didn't she? How could she not?

Maren took the pizza. "Did Polly tell you about her ribbon?"

I assumed only hookers or drug dealers were corrupt enough to be naked in front of people and not care. Apparently I was wrong. I had the strong urge to laugh. To bust up laughing. I clenched my jaw tight. Surely this was a joke, right? No one was laughing. No wonder Pete thought she was interesting. Interesting, naked—same difference.

"Yeah, she did," I said, remembering the ribbon's untimely death in the Cassinis' backyard. "That's great," I added, pretending I wasn't surrounded by a bunch of freaks.

"Next time she's going to get a blue ribbon, aren't you, Polly?"

"Gonna try," Polly said.

"Don't leave it up to fate, Polly. If you'd studied a little longer, you would've easily won first place."

Polly shrugged.

"You're smarter than any of those kids," her mother lectured, voice rising. "Besides, this camp is expensive. You need to show a little more initiative."

This naked woman was yelling at angelic Polly right

in front of me. No one was laughing. My jaw was clamped so tight I was forgetting to breathe. My mom wouldn't have mentioned a stupid ribbon; my mom didn't even know how to keep score in tennis. My mom wore clothes.

Polly changed the subject. "Where'd you guys go?"

Great, more conversation.

Maren spat out the details of the James Bond flick they'd seen. "The line was clear out to the parking lot, and we had to wait an hour for tickets . . ."

Meanwhile, Pete was falling asleep sitting up. Eyes closed, his head nodded. He'd catch himself only to dip down again. Finally, he shook off the sleep like a wet dog. Disgusted, he grabbed Maren's shirt from the floor and tossed it at her as she continued to talk about 007.

"It itches," she said, like he was stupid.

"There are other people here," he said, meaning me.

"So?" She flipped the blouse back to the floor.

"I'll get you a T-shirt."

"What are you, a Boy Scout all of a sudden?"

Their eyes locked. Pete looked away, preventing the impending fight.

"Anyway, the end of the movie was great because—"

Pete gripped Maren's shoulder. Her skin turned light pink from the pressure. He could have crushed her bones had he wanted to: he was that strong. I kind of wished he'd slug her or something. I already disliked her and I barely knew her. Pete looked at me apologetically.

"It's time for you girls to get some sleep, isn't it?"

We retreated, without snacks. I examined Polly's chameleon face for some kind of an explanation, like maybe she was adopted or something and not really human but an angel here to comfort me. Her face revealed nothing.

I snuggled into my sleeping bag, suddenly tired.

"Hall?" Polly whispered in the pitch-blackness.

"Huh?"

"Good night."

I lay awake for a while. My sleeping bag was too hot and I couldn't get comfortable. In the dark I somehow knew that Polly burying her ribbon and me slicing up my tennis academy catalogs hadn't really accomplished anything. I knew that, even if Polly didn't.

• Chapter Ten •

"**T**urn the sound down! I'm on the phone."

Brad played air guitar to the radio while my brothers' rude friends propped their feet on my mom's coffee table.

My mom refers to my brothers' friends as riffraff and hooligans, but Michael smiles and says, "But, Mom, they're harmless. Practically choirboys, even."

The Choirboys burped loudly while verbalizing their desire for some girl named Stacey. "The girl is hot. She is hotter than hot," Michael said.

Choirboy 1 said, "I'm not saying she's not *fine*. I'm saying what makes you think she'll date you?"

"Dream on," Choirboy 2 said. "She's too hot for you."

"No, she's too hot for *you*," Michael said.

"You're afraid to talk to her! She doesn't date mutes," Choirboy 2 said, letting out a belch that could have made it into *The Guinness Book of World Records*.

"I've talked to her plenty," Michael boasted.

"Yeah," said Choirboy 1. "You said, 'Excuse me.' Once. That's not a conversation."

"Turn it down! I'm telling Mom!" I screamed, my voice barely audible above the music.

Brad cut the sound and mimicked me. "I'm telling Mom . . . I'm telling Mom . . ."

The Choirboys laughed.

"Are you OK?" Eve said on the phone. "What's going on?"

"Nothing." Explaining my brothers was pointless. She lived in a girlie home where people said things like "Please" and "Thank you."

"Everyone's here. Where are you?"

"On my way."

Ms. Jensen met me at the door with her purse over her shoulder and keys in her hand. "Hello, Hall. The girls are on the back porch. I'll be home later to give everyone a ride home. You girls behave while I'm gone," she said. She obviously wasn't aware that we spent the majority of our waking hours inside her home.

"Yes," I assured her, "we will."

Melissa was crouched over, painting her toenails. Eve was supine, with a dusty pillow under her head. Only Polly bothered to greet me as I stepped onto the cool porch. She scooted over, making room for me on her lawn chair.

"Hey," she said, pushing her bangs out of her eyes, as she often did. I think she liked them long so she could fluff them up and push them out of her way. The repetitive act seemed to comfort the margins of her secretive soul. I simply could not figure the girl out.

"Anybody up for going to 7-Eleven?" Eve asked.

"I am," I said.

"Sure," Polly said.

Melissa looked a little worried. "It's a long way."

"Live a little, Melissa," Eve said. And that was that. We rose simultaneously.

Eve carted her new water bottle with her, handing it to Melissa as we spilled out onto the asphalt. Sidewalks were for dog walkers; we commanded the street, taking up half of it, walking in a line. Dusk had settled in. The air smelled sweet, clean.

Melissa clamped her teeth around the water bottle and tipped it.

"Don't laugh," I said, hoping to make her laugh.

Her lips pursed. She almost swallowed, but then she

105

couldn't. She doubled over, water flowing out of her mouth like a hydrant. Most of it landed on the front of Eve's cotton shorts, leaving a big mark. Eve looked at us, then at her shorts.

"Ew, gross!" Polly wailed.

"You know I didn't mean it, Eve," Melissa said.

Polly and I exchanged a pitying look. Then we burst out laughing.

Appalled by her bad luck, Eve danced around the pavement. "I'm gonna pee . . . *I'm gonna pee.*"

"Looks like you just did!" I said.

I loved these people.

From a distance, the 7-Eleven looked like a bug motel. Customers were sucked into the lit door and never seemed to come back out. I hate going to Sev with friends. The clerks assume we're there to steal. Even when we're paying for a Slurpee they act like we've shoved candy bars down our pants, planning to sell them for profit.

Our mission complete, we stepped back onto the asphalt, chewing nougat and drinking cold Big Gulps. I should've been eating something healthy that Trent would approve of. An apple or a banana. But I didn't feel like it.

I pointed to the darkening skies. "It's going to rain something fierce."

"Let's take the shortcut through the field," Eve suggested. "To the bluffs. They'll take us to Naples—from there it's five minutes."

"We better," Melissa said. "I don't want to get struck by lightning."

"Why don't we walk back up Maizeland Road the way we came?" asked Polly. "Where the streetlights are."

"Afraid of the boogeyman?" Eve taunted.

"No, booger."

"We don't have time to take Maizeland," I said. Eve was wrong, though—the empty field would indeed bring us to Naples Drive, but Naples Drive was a good fifteen minutes from being anywhere near her house. I had other motives. Luke Kimberlin's house was at 18 Naples Drive; I'd looked it up in the phone book.

The field was a nightmare. In the dark, we trampled tall weeds, struggling with the uneven ground. In the belly of the field our shoes sank in pockets of mud.

"Whose bright idea was this?" Polly said.

Eve huffed in response.

Weeds scratched our bare legs bloody. Crickets chirped like jet engines. Bugs propelled themselves, sucking, biting tender flesh. Crawling, creeping. Flying, landing. Bugs, bugs, everywhere bugs.

As usual, Eve stomped ahead of us, leading. I could barely keep up. The mud got deeper and deeper with each step.

"Quit stepping on my heels, Melissa," Eve yelled.

"But I can't see anything," Melissa moaned.

"Don't walk so fast, Eve," Polly said from behind me, breathless.

"*I'm* not walking fast, *you're* walking slow," Eve said.

I ignored the tempo of the others and tried concentrating on exactly where I was stepping. The girls were concerned with mud; I was concerned with mud leading to a sprained ankle, leading to a destroyed tennis game.

"Something is crawling in my hair! Get it out, get it out!" Polly cried.

I ran my hand over Polly's scalp. "It's gone now, whatever it was," I said.

"Does anyone else smell skunk?" Melissa asked.

We did, all of us. Eve busted into a full sprint; we were more than happy to follow, screaming. Dogs in the distance heard our hysteria and met our shrieks with long, low howls, as if they understood.

We finally reached Naples Drive and relaxed. Lights from distant homes were dim but appreciated. The air turned from calm to frigid. Rain was imminent.

Eve put her hand over her heart, dumbfounded. "Wait, we're going the wrong direction!"

"Don't look at me," Melissa said. "I'm following you."

"We're *all* following you," Polly said as she reached down and scraped mud splatter from her calves. "Any more great suggestions, Eve?" she asked.

"No one made you come with us," Eve said, her tone hostile, biting. "You could've walked up Maizeland Road by yourself if you wanted."

"Alone? In the dark? Thanks!" Polly said, and started laughing, maybe at Eve, maybe at the mud she now flung off her hands.

"So shut up," Eve said.

I whipped my head over to Eve. Polly wasn't saying anything the rest of us weren't feeling. "Shut up" wasn't necessary. Polly stopped laughing and straightened her body. "You shut up," she said, challenging Eve.

Eve stared at her. The space between us became brittle, heavy.

Melissa looked to me to save us all. I was sick of the drama. "Why don't both of you shut up? I'm not backtracking through the field," I said. "Let's go. We're wasting time."

It wasn't long before we saw two figures underneath a streetlight. "It's Luke and Bruce," I whispered. "Don't look, don't look. Oh no."

The boys were trying to maim each other. The Greek God flailed crusty pinecones at Bruce, who, ducking behind shrubs to gather his own ammunition, flung them back with surprising accuracy.

Luke paused, shielding his eyes from the glare of the streetlight. "Holloway?"

In a matter of seconds we stood with them underneath the misty light. Bruce Weissman was Luke's best friend. He lived along Naples Drive, attended Westland Prep, and belonged to the country club, like Luke. Polly stood suspiciously close to him, ignoring everyone else, filling the air with small talk. Her eyes were brightly lit, like a Christmas tree.

Eve stared at Bruce and Polly. I had no idea why. I bumped Eve and nodded toward Luke. I turned so no one else would hear, searching for her opinion. She touched the tip of her finger to her nose, concealing its four freckles. "Why does *he* like *you*?" she whispered, sounding nonchalant.

The cruelty of that floored me, even if it was exactly what I'd asked myself a million times. Eve probably didn't mean it with malice, but still. "Why wouldn't he?" I whispered back, echoing Polly's previous take on the situation.

Luke edged toward his iron driveway gate and motioned for me to join him. "Hey, Holloway," he said.

110

"Hey." I scooted near him and placed my hand on the cold wrought iron bars, balancing myself as I stomped some mud from my shoes.

"You guys just come from the field?"

"We were trying to take a shortcut. I don't recommend it unless you like mud," I said.

"Thanks for the heads-up."

He slid his fingers through his hair. A cool breeze melted into my skin. Part of his sleeve touched my arm. It was perfect. I wasn't quite as nervous as I had been the first time he talked to me at the club. That could've been a fluke; this wasn't. He *wanted* to talk to me. But the sense of danger, of risk, of peril still pressed into me—like anything could happen at any moment. Parts of my insides sparked. If that was love, I was *in it*.

"Do you always walk by my house in the dark?" he kidded.

"Don't you wish."

"Yeah, I do. Next time come in. Scale the wall."

"Ha, ha," I said sarcastically.

"Ha to you, Holloway."

It was more than perfect.

"Those are your friends?"

"Uh-huh."

He glanced over at them, looking them up and down. "Well, Polly is OK, I guess."

"Yeah, Polly is . . . cool," I said.

I glanced through the iron gate. Yard lights illuminated the lawn. The driveway curved, making only a corner of the garage visible through the landscaping. I guess they didn't want poor people looking at their house.

The wind picked up. Swirling gusts swept toward us. "Hall?" Eve said. "We should go."

Bruce stepped away from Polly and hopped on his bike. "Yeah, Luke, I gotta go, too."

"OK," Luke said to Bruce, "see you tomorrow." He turned to the girls. "Holloway will catch up in a minute."

My muddy friends started walking. Polly shot me a look of glee.

Luke grabbed my wrist. "I have to tell you something."

"What? Are you going to throw a pinecone at me?"

He was in my face all of a sudden, his lips pressed to mine. Luke Kimberlin was *kissing* me! It was a blur of details: the smell of rain not yet fallen, the proximity of his excellent forehead. His lips were rough, like they hadn't had ChapStick in years. He stuck his tongue in my mouth. I didn't know what to do, so I stuck my tongue in his mouth. Then my lips made a stupid smacking noise.

Suddenly Luke backed away.

My mind was spinning, spinning, spinning into some bright place, a place of excellence, of joy.

"That's what I had to tell you," he said, letting go of my wrist. The warmth of his hand stayed with me for a few seconds and then escaped into the night air, gone forever.

"I gotta go," I said.

He unlatched the heavy gate. "Bye," he called.

"Bye, Luke."

Ping-Pong-ball-sized raindrops fell: one on my nose, one on my knee, a few on my arm. A grand total of ten socked me by the time I caught up with the girls.

"What happened?" Polly asked.

"You won't believe what happened—"

"It's going to hail," Eve said, cutting me off, taking charge, her reason perfectly legitimate. "We better run the rest of the way. We've got to get back before my mom does."

We took off down the street, Eve first. The sky lit. A roll of thunder cracked into the black night. The heavens opened and rain pounded down. Eve's lungs let loose a battle cry as she increased her pace. Melissa whimpered a little, trying to protect her head from the rain while running at full speed.

Polly jogged next to me with a slower gait, fearless of the elements, fearless of Eve, fearless. She seized my elbow. "I don't want to wait. Tell me what happened, Hall."

We hit a streetlight just then, and with her eyes on my face, I puckered my lips and pretended to kiss the rain. Her face got jovial. "No!" she said.

"Yes," I said.

Eve was too far ahead of us to know or care. And for some reason I didn't care that Polly heard my news first, either.

• Chapter Eleven •

The Fourth of July arrived without much fanfare. My parents invited friends over for a barbecue. Michael and Brad were in high spirits. The Fourth of July is their favorite holiday, surpassing Christmas, even. Anything involving fire or explosives gets my brothers' immediate and unrelenting attention.

Anyway, Eve was the only one of my friends who could come; the other girls had family plans. She and I lit sparklers, sipped lemonade, and ate burgers off my parents' new grill (they bought the grill with money from the Dead Grandpa Bonus Fund; I spared her the story). She pelted me with a zillion questions about Bruce, out of nowhere: "How long have Bruce and Luke been friends? . . . Where *is* Bruce's house, anyway? . . . Do you think he's taller than Luke, or shorter? I'm thinking taller . . ."

I had no answers. And I thought she was joking, really. That night we'd seen them on the street it was clear Polly liked Bruce. Eve had stood back, silent. She'd *watched* Polly flirt with him.

"Let's go to Naples Drive," Eve suggested.

"Right now? Why?"

"Maybe Bruce is riding his bike. If Luke likes you, maybe Bruce will like me."

"Oh." I didn't have the heart to tell her that Polly had already spent a solid hour on the phone with me gushing about Bruce. On the other hand, I didn't know if Bruce liked her back. So I uneasily said, "Sure, let's go."

With feelings of fear and fun, we pedaled our bikes to Naples Drive. Though sounds of elegant parties floated over the walled estates, the street was void of life. Still, the possibility of encountering Bruce made Eve giddy for some reason. It took me a moment to gather my feelings about it.

"Let's go, Eve. He isn't here."

"Want to bike up to Grandview Overlook?" she asked.

I didn't feel like trailing her bike up the brutal road, even for the stellar view at the top. It wouldn't be a casual ride, it'd be a race.

"Not really," I said. "The hill is too steep. Let's go to the stables again—that's an easy ride."

"Good enough," she said, and started pedaling.

Boom. She was gone.

"Eve," I hollered.

She kept going. Faster, even. We zoomed by my practice court and the Benet Hill Center. I thought for sure she'd look back and answer me. I thought wrong.

"Eve! Slow down!"

Cars whizzed past me. I was stuck riding on the edge of crumbling pavement so I wouldn't get hit. "Eve! Wait up!"

I was screaming. She had to have heard.

I finally caught up to her at the stables when she took a breather under a mighty oak. I heaved for oxygen, unable to catch my breath, feeling nauseous.

Several potholes had been filled recently. The scent of fresh asphalt and tar nearly knocked me over.

Eve took a whiff of the stale air. "Not one of your greatest ideas, Hall," she said, sounding irritated.

"What's the matter with you?" I said. "Didn't you hear me calling you for three miles? Can't we just ride bikes like normal people once in a while? It's not a race!"

"I felt like going fast. Sue me," she scoffed. "You're the athlete. What, you can't keep up?"

"Riding a bike isn't a competition. It's *supposed* to be for fun," I accused.

Eve looked off at the empty horse trails on the bluffs as if fascinated by them in some way.

"Besides, what do you care about me being an athlete? You never even watch me play."

"You know I hate sports. They're boring."

"*They* are or *I* am? Polly watched me practice serves, and she isn't my best friend, you are."

I used to cherish Eve for never talking about tennis or wanting to watch me play. But to Polly it was no big deal—why *wouldn't* she be interested in my game? We were friends. In comparison, Eve's disregard for it just seemed selfish.

"I don't give a crap what Polly does," she said flatly.

"Then why are you trying to steal Bruce from her?"

Her jaw dropped. Disgust flooded her pale features. "Since when do I need Polly's *permission* to like someone? Or yours?"

"You and I have seen Luke and Bruce around the neighborhood for, like, over a year. You never *once* mentioned that you liked Bruce until you saw Polly talking to him that night on Naples Drive. You don't find that bizarre?"

The rims of her eyes turned pink like she might cry.

Eve never cried. She was truly hurt. That killed me. I hadn't really meant to pick a fight.

"I liked him *way* before that," she said. "I'm sick of bike riding. I'm going home," she announced.

"Wait," I pleaded.

"What?"

"I'll talk to Luke," I offered, forcing the words from my mouth. "Maybe Bruce does like you." What was I saying? I'd swallowed all common sense. "I'll ask Luke about it next time I see him. I promise."

Eve softened. She nodded a little. "OK," she said, her eyes returning to their normal color. "Yeah, ask Luke."

She calmly turned her bike around.

"Eve, do you actually like him?"

"I just said I did," she said, and took off, back the way we'd come, first, first, always first, expecting me to follow. I couldn't blame her for being upset. I'd neglected Eve for weeks; she only just now made the connection. Eve's distress seemed more about Polly than Bruce. But did Eve dislike Polly because I liked her *first,* or because I liked her *at all?*

Days later, I found a note in my tennis bag at the country club. It said: *Holloway, meet me in your yard at ten tonight. Don't get caught. Luke.*

My obsession, like a pigeon, had come home to roost.

It was inexplicably easy to sneak out of my house. I took a bunch of dramatic precautions anyway: yawned, rubbed my eyes, told my family (like they cared) I was gonna turn in early. When the moment arrived, my parents were in bed and my brothers were comatose in front of the blaring TV. I could've had a double life as a burglar; no one would've noticed.

I eased the back door open. Luke stood in the middle of the deck, waiting. In plain view. The deck light shining on him! Fear was a fist squeezing my heart. Was he stupid?

"Are you crazy? What are you doing?"

"Hi," he said.

"Shh!"

He grabbed my hand and we crept into the cool night air. Luke holding my hand was like me serving an ace: I knew it was a possibility, but it still thrilled me when it happened. The fragrance of mowed lawns filled our nostrils.

When we reached the entrance to Naples Drive Luke got quiet, whispering his words, the nearness of his own house making him cautious. "Holloway . . . I like that name . . . Holloway."

"Only 'cause you don't have to live with it."

"Sounds like an actress. You could win an Oscar with a name like that."

I chuckled. "Thanks. I mean—I'd like to thank the

Academy . . ." But the only academy edging into my future was the tennis kind.

"My sister, Stacey, is watching our neighbors' house. They're in Europe for the whole summer—"

"Your sister's name is Stacey? Stacey Kimberlin?"

"The one and only."

"My brothers are in love with your sister. All their friends are, too."

"Everybody loves Stacey," the Greek God stated. "She's got a boyfriend; she's only seventeen, but he's a freshman in college. Anyway, she's watching our neighbors' house for the summer, and I know where she hides the key. That's where we're going."

"Cool."

When Luke mentioned scaling the wall he wasn't kidding. We reached the gate north of his and scanned the premises like deviants, watching for headlights.

"You first." He knelt down, intertwining his fingers to make a human step. I stepped in, resting my hand on his head until I got my balance. I propelled myself, skinning my wrist on the wall.

Oh no. Not my wrist. I needed my wrist to serve, to hit overheads, to hit anything. The Cherry Creek Invitational was tomorrow. Injure *anything* but my wrist—my thigh, my back, my neck . . . not my wrist! I checked it for blood. There wasn't any. It'd be OK. It would have to be.

"Don't worry," Luke said as he shoved me over, his hands on my butt, "they don't have dogs."

The drop was a good six feet. My grip slipped. "Oh crap." My ankles hit the ground and buckled, making me topple over. I stayed in the grass, resting my hands on the cool earth, wondering if I was hurt. "Ouch!"

"Quiet!" he warned from the other side of the wall.

My ankle. One of them. The left one. Was it tender or twisted? Tender or broken? Tender or beyond repair? I moved it around in circles. The muscles loosened. Just tender. Only tender. Be fine by tomorrow. In good shape for the tournament. Thank God for tender.

"Do you need help?" I asked.

"No, I got it, watch out," he whispered. He fell into the grass beside me.

We picked ourselves up off the ground. The estate was flawless, with a lawn the size of a football field. Rows of tiny cone-shaped trees aligned themselves along the driveway. The porch light was a beacon.

I said something incredibly intelligent, like, "Wow. That's the house? What if they have an alarm system?"

"Shh!" he ordered. "Someone might hear."

I trailed Luke through a garden to the indoor pool, attatched to the main house. I tried to see the Greek

God's house, without luck; the stucco walls were too high.

"Come on, Holloway."

"I can't see you, it's so dark."

"I'm right here." He waved his hand. I felt him fanning air at me more than I could see his fingers.

At the base of the pool house's French doors lay a welcome mat. Kneeling down, Luke slid his hand underneath it, scraping the pulp of his fingertips along the flagstone until we heard a slight ping. Smiling, he held the key close to my face so I could witness the glory. Presto, we were in. It was that simple.

The pool's tile was dark, making the water look deep blue, like a lagoon. We kept the lights low so as not to be discovered. "Nice, huh?" Luke said.

"Yeah. Are you sure we won't—"

"Shh!"

My heart inflated. I wasn't that nervous around Luke particularly—but I definitely was about our circumstances. This element of danger, this click of peril fizzed inside me. If the owners of the house came back early, like right *now,* could I run fast enough to get away?

A slight cracking noise progressed across the room. We stopped cold. "What's that?" I asked.

"Shh."

"Let's go, Luke. *Please.*"

He grabbed hold of my arm to keep me from bolting out the door.

"Luke—"

"Anybody there?" he said.

No response. *Anybody there?* What deranged killer would be polite enough to respond to that question?

"Luke, please."

"Shh! Wait a sec."

I backed up, positioning myself to run. "Are they home?" I asked.

"No, look." Luke pointed at the many long windows. "The wind," he said. "It's just the wind." The moonlight proved him right: the leaves of aspen trees danced like clumsy ballerinas in the breeze, smacking against the windowpanes.

I exhaled. "Yes, wind."

"Want to swim?" Luke asked, happy now.

"No suit." I couldn't jump in with all my clothes on. If I had to walk home in sopping wet clothes I'd probably catch pneumonia and die in the middle of the night. I'd fail to show up at the Cherry Creek tournament in the morning. Coach would come looking for me. Stand over my deathbed. Raise me from the dead. Make me run sprints. And then kill me himself for my complete irresponsibility.

Still, I wanted to be here. With Luke.

"I guess I could leave my T-shirt on. And take off my shorts . . . but you can't look," I said.

"I'll get stuff to eat." He passed the wicker furniture at the far end of the room and disappeared into the main house's kitchen.

I shimmied out of my shorts. Crap—I was wearing ratty old Christmas underwear. Rudolph the Red-Nosed Reindeer covered the waistband. Half of my butt hung out the back. I made a mental note to throw them away when I got home.

I dipped a toe in the water. It was frigid; I'd have to jump in or I'd lose my nerve. Closing my eyes, I took a leap. Water struck my skin like a thousand needles. I was frozen but relieved: once I was in, the water was dark enough that I couldn't see anything *but* water. I wouldn't have to explain my stupid underwear to Luke.

I wasn't sure why Luke had brought me here, but I hoped we were going to kiss again. It would officially be kiss number 2. I was keeping count. I had a great need for more kissing. I didn't quite have the hang of it yet.

"Are you in?" Luke called. That was polite of him—to ask instead of vying for a glance at my butt.

"Yeah," I called.

The Greek God entered, arms piled with a box of

powdered-sugar doughnuts and cold sodas. I felt a pang for Melissa, being surrounded by the great snacks and all. "Want to eat now?" he asked.

"In a minute."

He set our feast on a wooden table, flung off his shirt, left his shorts on, and did a backflip into the pool, splashing me.

"Are you surprised?" he asked when he came up for air.

"Definitely surprised."

"Can't tell anyone. Stacey will freak if she knows we're here. I'll be grounded forever."

"I won't tell," I said. "Hey, can I ask you something that's none of my business?"

"Go for it."

"Did you really put whipped cream on the vice principal's car at Westland?"

A mouthful of water choked him. "How'd you know?"

"It's a rumor going around."

"Yeah," he said. "Actually, me and two other friends. But they didn't get caught, and I didn't want to tell on them. It wasn't even my idea," he said in his own defense. "It was stupid. His car was in the teachers' parking lot when we did it."

I moved my legs up and down, marching underwater. The water felt like ice cubes. My body tensed up. My ankle had stopped aching, though. No tenderness, even. Too frozen to feel pain. "It was stupid because his car was in the teachers' parking lot or because you did it at all?"

He raised his head, like he hadn't given it *that* much thought. "Both, I guess."

"So you got suspended, not expelled, right? You're still going to Westland next year?" I asked.

"Yes," he said, making a face. "It's a tough school. There's so much homework it's hard to keep up sometimes."

"Hmmm."

We made our way into the deep end. I hung on to the edge of the pool with numb fingers. I was relieved he wasn't an actual juvenile delinquent. He was more carefree than troubled.

He got out of the pool, his waterlogged shorts heavy and pulling on his waist, but quickly dove back in as goose bumps formed. "Oh, by the way, Bruce likes Polly," he said, surfacing, treading water.

Ugh. I'd almost forgotten my promise to Eve. "Are you sure? Eve sort of has a crush on him," I humbly said.

"Who's Eve?"

"The blond girl you met when we saw you that night. Blue eyes. Pale skin. Looks Norwegian. Super nice."

"Well, he likes Polly."

"Maybe he could like Eve instead," I said, and then laughed at myself. What a stupid thing to say.

Luke grinned, noting the absurdity. "He likes Polly. In fact, he went to the movies with her this afternoon."

"He did?" I'd definitely have to call Polly and get the gossip. I wondered why she hadn't called me, but I'd been in and out all day—to the club and the practice court—and my brothers weren't the best at giving me messages. I was both delighted for Polly and sad for Eve. But Eve couldn't accuse me of not trying. I'd told her I'd ask about it, and I had.

Luke swam to me and held on to the edge, his hand touching mine. Kissing was bound to happen. I wiped chlorine water from my lips.

He leaned toward me.

"So tell me about your trophies," he said.

"Huh?"

"Your tennis trophies. You've got, like, seven in that case at the club."

"You counted them?"

He nodded and moved his hand so it no longer touched mine. He looked at our awaiting snacks, solemn. "I used to be on the chess team at Westland. I was the captain. I was good. We went to state one year. We won."

What was he getting at? Who cared about trophies? My lips were officially numb from this freezing water. *Kiss me!* "So you have trophies?" I asked.

"Had," he admitted. "I quit the team. My friends made fun of me. Called me a chess wuss. Even Bruce. It's not cool to be on the chess team," he said, still not looking at me.

Apparently, this was a big box of pain to Luke and he'd chosen me as his confessional.

"You should play chess if you want to. If Bruce is your best friend, he'll understand, right?" I said. I thought about Eve. She'd never understood my tennis. She'd never been supportive. Who was I to give advice?

Luke got silent. Looked at me. "Maybe."

"No, really. You could make it cool. Especially if you win."

He laughed at that. "Well, you should know about winning," he said.

"Yeah, I guess." I was suddenly depressed. I'd be lucky to get five hours of sleep before the first match of my tournament tomorrow. I didn't want to face that tournament on eight hours of sleep, much less five. I shouldn't have come here. I let myself fall into the water and come back up. I swear my earlobes had icicles hanging off them. The water-laden walk home wasn't going to be fun.

"Bruce and I will be at the club tomorrow. Will you?" Luke asked.

"No, I have a tournament in Denver all week. The Cherry Creek Invitational."

He looked blank.

"I'm supposed to win it. I won it last year."

He leaned in and kissed my purple numb lips. Quick. No tongue. I'd risked pneumonia for that kiss.

"Good luck," he said, and then proclaimed, "race you!" He took off across the pool, navy blue water splashing every which way. I probably could've beaten him, but my green T-shirt was full of water and weighed me down like an anchor.

I knew what I had to do.

I heaved myself out of the pool, quickly grabbed my shorts, and yanked them on while water drained off my body as if I was a faucet.

Luke reached the opposite edge and looked around, expecting me by his side. He turned in the water and faced me, confused. My pruney feet shivered in a puddle of water. My shorts were already drenched and sticking to my legs.

"What are you doing?" Luke asked.

"I gotta go," I called across the water.

"Right now?" he said.

"Yeah, I have to be up at five a.m. to drive to Denver. Sorry," I said, and squeezed a bucketful of water out of my hair.

Forget walking home—I planned on running.

• Chapter Twelve •

Expectations kill tennis players. Happens all the time. Expectations rob the player of joy. A game? Who says this is a game? This is no game. High expectations turn the joy into pressure. The pressure festers and causes doubt, fear, causes a player to choke—to horribly lose a match she could've easily won. Expectations. Slow suffocation. Expectations laugh. Giggle. They mock me.

I win against a better player. Relief for a day. Only a day. Then pressure. Never lose to that player again. What's the problem? Go up in the rankings, not down. At any cost. No matter the cost. What is the cost? I will pay anything. Pay an arm? Leg? My soul?

Expectations come to steal my soul. Expectations shove their fist down my throat and tear out my soul. I give it gladly. Try to appease. Ask for rain. I will be soulless and not complain.

Expectations curse the core of me. Feel them in my bones. They *are* my bones. Gnawing on my joints. Cracking into splinters. Sucking out the marrow. Broken bones ground to powder.

The catch? Yes, the catch! Expectations are never pleased. Fulfill expectations and the expectations rise. Refuse to be satisfied. They want more. More wins. Trophies. More Holloway Braxton, goddess of the tennis world. Pay more. Be more. Suffer more. Claw my way to be ranked in the top four. *Only four?* What's the matter? Why not three, two, one? Won. She won, didn't she? Wasn't this supposed to be fun?

The Cherry Creek Invitational is a six-day tournament with players from Colorado and the surrounding states participating. My mom drove me to Denver the first two days. I went without protest, but things were definitely wrong. Very wrong. I was making obvious mistakes. A missed serve here, a long return there—it adds up. The sum of it is *losing*.

As my mom watched proudly in the stands

(*proudly*—gag!), I beat my opponents, but with tremendous effort. The scores were 6–4, 7–6 . . . I choked. Big-time.

On the third, fourth, and fifth days, Trent and his wife, Annie, drove me. I hoped having Trent close to me would spark my mind to its former ease. It didn't. Each match, against girls I'd beaten many times before, was a war. During changeovers, I gulped water like a fish. My feet were lead. This easy tournament was dismantling me.

Trent was clueless. He was so used to me winning that he and Annie skipped my matches in order to hob-nob with other coaches and spouses. I knew he hadn't been watching because he was *congratulating* me on my wins.

On the day of the final we were driving on High-way 25 north to Cherry Creek. It was 6:30 a.m., the air outside was clear and dewy, the sun not yet bright.

I stared at the back of Coach's head: it was smooth like a river rock. That comforted me. Soothed my nerves. I've spent weeks of my life, months probably, staring at his head on the way to tournaments, and he's none the wiser. I don't want to suck at this game. I want to win, only win, and stare at the back of his head and be comforted.

Energy always encompasses Coach on the way to a

tournament. He's electric. Full of cheer. My theory is that sometime in his early life Trent wanted to be a player rather than a coach. Maybe in the car he believes *he's* the player—that's why all the cheer. His cheer is a fact rather than an emotion. The hulking relentless man is not emotional. I found myself wishing I could touch my fingers to his temple and capture the cheer. I wondered if it could be held in the palm of my hand as if it was a bird or a penny.

Annie turned in her seat, smiling.

"What?" I asked.

"Nothing."

"Uh-huh, what?"

"Give her the present already," Trent said.

"What present? What?"

"I don't know," Annie said. "I should wait. This is a victory present; there hasn't been a victory yet."

"A simple matter of time. Are you winning today, Hall?" Coach asked.

"Yes," I lied. When did I become such a liar?

Annie was cool. Her skin was the same milk chocolate color as Trent's, but hers looked like velvet. She produced a plastic bag from the floorboard and handed it to me. "Hall, I can't wait for you to see this!"

I turned the bag upside down, dumping the contents

into my lap. And there it was. A cloth Swiss flag. Bigger than a beach towel. My mood lifted. I almost had cheer. "Annie—you didn't!"

"I did," she said, all smiles. Trent watched my expression from the rearview mirror.

"Annie, Annie, Annie! This is so great. I'll hang it on my bedroom wall. Thanks, Annie!"

"No problem." She turned to Trent. "Can't deny it, the girl's got good taste."

"Not interested in her taste, interested in her *game.*"

"*I'm* interested in your taste, Hall," Annie said.

I don't see Annie much, only during tournaments. She's nice in a way that isn't like a mom but more like a friend. I never feel like a junior player when I'm around Annie. I feel like a pro.

The only sport Annie likes is shopping, and my tournaments give her great opportunities, especially the ones in different states. Nevada, Utah, Florida, Arizona: she's there, credit card in hand. Last February, when Janie and I played our one measly international tournament in Mexico and got slammed by our opponents (Janie by a German and me by an Argentinean), Annie consoled us with sombreros purchased from the hotel gift shop.

At smaller, local tournaments like this one she often

buys me Slurpees on the drive home and we discuss our crush on Roger Federer. He's a pro player from Switzerland. We call him King Roger because he rules the court like royalty. He's an all-court player who hits the ever-living guts out of the ball. If he's struggling, he keeps it inside, plays it cool, never lets his opponent see anything but strength. It's only after he's won a difficult point or game that he'll raise his hands overhead and let out a wicked roar of a yell. Only then is it evident he was unsure of the outcome.

In the blazing heat he wears zinc oxide on his nose and cheekbones to stave off the sun. I love it when he does that. He's a warrior, like me.

Annie calls Roger Federer luscious. Wisely, she says it only when Trent is out of carshot. I'm pretty sure she wants a Swiss flag for herself as well, but Trent wouldn't be too keen on that. Coach isn't the kind of man who wants his wife thinking other men are luscious.

"I bought Trent a Swiss Army knife at the mall and it sparked my imagination. I knew you wouldn't want weaponry, but I wanted to get you something with a Swiss theme," Annie said, referring to the flag.

"Let it inspire you, Hall," Trent said. "Be soaked in inspiration."

"This is fantastic."

"You like it, then, Chickadee?" she said.

"Like it? I love it!"

"Good."

I got worried for a second. "And if I lose today?" I said, my voice cracking.

"Lose?" Annie said.

"Lose?" Coach said.

"You know, fail to win?"

"That'll be the day," Coach said, shaking his head.

I felt ill.

Coaches aren't allowed to offer advice during a match. Instead they sit in the stands, recording the mistakes their particular player makes. Trent brought his notebook; it was the first thing he grabbed when he got out of the car. He planned on watching every bit of the final.

My opponent, from Utah, was Hanna Scott. I play her constantly. I beat her in the quarterfinals of the USTA National Opens and in the semifinal at the Copper Bowl, but she beat me the four tournaments before that. She's ranked higher, number two, in the Girls 14's.

Crowds love Hanna Scott. She's a vision. A beauty. Perfect blond ringlets of hair. Textbook ringlets. Angelic face. Great serve. Hard serve. Rich. Spoiled. Brat. Hanna Scott. Her name alone makes me cringe. The girl is everything I'm not. Little Miss Perfect. Little Miss Popular. Hanna Scott. I want to break her racquet, render her helpless. Break her into bits and pieces, into spare parts. Dumb perfect curls. Stupid perfect face. Great serve. Amazing serve. Jealous of the serve. The bane of my existence, Hanna Scott.

Hanna Scott hates volley players. Sometimes if I rush the net she'll choke and hit a bad shot. I prayed she'd be weak. Prayed that if I attacked the net she'd *give* me the points. I took my place at the baseline. The crowd clapped enthusiastically for Hanna Scott. They would.

Thump . . . thump . . . thump . . . She won the point. Damn. She was better than I remembered, or maybe I was worse.

Thump . . . thump . . .

Squinting, I could barely see the ball. It was invisible. No one else seemed to notice.

Thump . . . thump . . .

. . . thump . . . thump . . . thump . . .

"Scott leads one game to love," the umpire said.

I paused to wipe sweat from my brow. I studied my racquet strings, rearranging them slightly, desperate to find my rhythm. *Breathe,* I told myself, *breathe.* I tried to hit the angle. Open the court. Take the point. It backfired. She whacked it hard, whizzed it past me, for a winner.

139

. . . *thump* . . . "Agg!" I lost another point.

Bouncing up and down, I warmed my muscles, shaking tension from my bones.

. . . *thump* . . . Out!

It kept going badly: an unlucky streak of misery.

"Scott leads three games to love," the umpire announced. Did he have to say it so loud?

We returned to our chairs for a changeover break.

Trent wrote furiously in his notebook. The crowd was fidgety and unimpressed with the lopsided match. They wanted blood; I was giving weakness.

"Time," the chair umpire called.

I tied my shoe, giving myself an extra moment to think. What was I doing wrong? What command would Trent bellow? I closed my eyes and waited. I got a slight echo, but it was muffled and mixed, out of my grasp. My head ached. My guts void. My game vanished.

Should I attack the net? Hit to her backhand? Fear swelled in my muscles: between my shoulders and at my ankles. If I couldn't win a stupid Cherry Creek tournament, how could I hack it at a tennis academy like Bickford? *Trent, where are you?* I waited. Nothing. Pressure. Fear. *Speak to me, Trent, speak to me . . .*

The revelation rolled over me like a bulldozer.

Trent's voice was gone.

It was never coming back.

Ever.

"Time," the umpire called again.

My head spun. My hands sweat from fear. I rocked back and forth at the baseline, awaiting Hanna's serve.

Trent's voice was gone.

It was never coming back.

Ever.

It was one thing to hate the thought of Bickford, to want to stay in Colorado and be a champion. It was something else entirely for Coach's voice to wither and die. Without his voice, I wouldn't be a champion *anywhere*. Suddenly Bickford Tennis Academy was the least of my worries.

Hanna bounced the ball. I swallowed hard.

As Hanna brought her racquet back, her grip was awkward. I could tell even across the court. She hit the ball . . . *thud* . . . then recoiled in pain. Her titanium racquet fell to the court.

My prayers were answered.

Hanna looked at the umpire. "I need an injury time-out," she said, mouth hanging open in disgust.

"Three minutes," the umpire called.

The staff trainer hustled courtside, barking for information. Hanna held out her thumb, as if to say, *Duh!* He produced balm that reeked so much I could smell it the instant he unscrewed the cap. Hanna stared straight ahead, dead to everything except her desire to get back on court and beat the living daylights out of me.

Unsatisfied, the trainer strapped tape on Hanna's appendage. Everyone knows thumbs can't be taped. Thumbs have to be flexible to serve. To heck with Hanna Scott and her stupid thumb—now I had a chance to win. A sprained thumb can cause damage!

"Time," the umpire called.

Hanna whimpered.

Thump . . . She hit the ball into the net. *Thump* . . . Again, into the net. *Bounce, bounce, bounce . . . thump . . .* Into the net. She double-faulted, one, two, three, four times in a row. I won a game from her double faults. It was a miracle!

Thump . . . thump . . . Out! When she finally got it over the net, it was out!

Come on, Hall, I thought. All I had to do was get the ball over the net and Hanna's sore thumb would do the rest. What more could I ask? The game proceeded, with me winning one clumsy point after another. She gave up altogether and glanced at her parents in the stands.

"I can't play," she said politely. "Hurts too much."

The crowd voiced one collective *ooh* for Hanna Scott

and her brave effort. I exhaled. If one player can't continue, the other player wins.

"Three games to one, Hanna Scott retires. Hall Braxton wins," the umpire announced, confirming.

The crowd gave me sparse applause. Technically I'd won, but everyone knew it was an ugly win. Hanna and I didn't shake hands at the net, what with her thumb and all. Just as well. I didn't want her congratulations. I felt like a total fraud.

As the officials prepared to hand me the trophy, I looked for Trent. As he closed his notebook, his eyes burned into me. I would pay for this display of my declining tennis abilities, of that I was certain.

The car ride home was less than fun. Apparently Trent thought I'd been trying to *humiliate* Hanna Scott. Since I'd beaten her at previous tournaments, Coach thought I was showing off at my opponent's expense—prolonging the match, delaying the points, in order to show up her tennis skills. He thought I'd been *pretending* to play badly! It didn't occur to him that expectations and his absent voice were crumbling my game. It didn't occur to him I sucked.

Coach half watched the road and half craned his neck around to yell. His shaved head glistened with sweat. Sportsmanship was a big deal.

"Confidence is one thing, but arrogance is something else. I *never* want to see that kind of spoiled-brat behavior again. Are you listening, Hall?"

"Yeah."

"Well?"

"I'm not a spoiled brat. I'm the least spoiled brat out there." It was true. Spoiled brats packed the junior circuit. Some of them were such spoiled brats they threw tantrums when they didn't win.

"What would you call it, then?"

I looked out the window, letting the highway asphalt blur my vision. "I don't know."

"You don't know? *You don't know?* Do you think Kim Clijsters became a top-ten player by having a bad attitude?"

"No," I said weakly.

"Do you think Maria Sharapova won Wimbledon at seventeen, before she even graduated from high school, because she has attitude problems?"

"No."

"Do you think your darling Roger Federer wins Slams over and over and over again, *making history,* because his attitude needs adjusting?"

I felt the fabric of my Swiss flag, refusing to feel guilty.

"You're out there to do your best, not taunt the other

players with mind games. When you're that much better than an opponent, you win quickly, not obscenely. What have I told you about winning graciously?"

"If you can't win graciously, you don't deserve to win."

"Did you deserve to win today?"

I didn't answer.

His chest heaved. *"Did you deserve to win?"*

"No."

"You better believe you didn't. Never in my life have I seen such arrogance on a tennis court."

Annie put her hand on his shoulder, signaling him to shut up. He got quiet.

Winning graciously, ha! This same man repeated my warrior story to whoever would listen. Apparently, slamming a tennis ball into an opponent and breaking her arm was OK, but humiliating an opponent (which I wasn't doing) was unsportsmanlike. Whatever. That's the bad thing about adults; even the good ones like Trent change the rules without warning in order to fill some obscure need for control. It seemed he was pretty much being a hypocrite, but what do I know?

Trent's voice was gone.

It was never coming back.

Ever.

Without his voice I didn't trust myself on the court.

145

Without trust it was impossible to acquire a blank head. Without trust there was nothing. I rode along in the backseat, my eyes fixed on the bright color of my Swiss flag. I was numb from the top of my head to the tips of my toes, and I thought, *This must be what nothing feels like.*

• Chapter Thirteen •

"**H**ow was the tournament?" Eve asked over the phone. It was out of character for her to mention tennis. I wondered if she was doing it to compete with Polly on some level.

"Huh? Oh, I won."

"You always win. What's new?"

"No I don't."

"Yeah, right. You've got it made."

"What's that supposed to mean?"

"Can't you take a compliment? I'm just saying you always win."

I let it go. She didn't understand, and I didn't expect her to. None of my friends, not even Polly, knew about the possibility of Bickford Tennis Academy looming in my future, mainly because I didn't want to have to discuss it night and day.

"So, what did you find out?" she asked.

"About what?"

"You said you'd ask Luke if Bruce likes me. Don't tell me you forgot."

I'd hoped to avoid this conversation. Eve had decency, which meant a lot to me but was staggeringly unimportant to other people. Why couldn't Bruce open his dumb eyes, see Eve was pretty like Norway, and like her?

"No, I didn't forget," I said, racking my brain for an elegant way to crush her.

"So . . . ?"

"Well, um, Bruce kind of likes Polly."

"When did all this happen?"

"I don't know. After we saw them on the street that night, I guess."

"But you knew I liked him. *I told you.* I can't believe you didn't tell Polly to back off. How could you do that to me?"

"Well, why didn't *you* tell her?" I said in my own defense.

"Because I told *you.*"

"Well, it's not my fault he doesn't like you."

I knew the minute I said it that I shouldn't have.

"Do you think I'm stupid? I see you walking home from *her* house all the time. You're too busy with Polly to be bothered with me. I thought I was your best friend!"

"You are."

"Liar," she said. The phone went dead.

I called her back, but she refused to answer. Out of guilt I got on my bike and trekked down Wynkoop Drive to talk to her face to face. She'd have to answer the door. I rang the bell once politely, then assaulted it twenty times in frustration. Curtains in the living room window rustled—Eve pretending she wasn't home.

My plans of apology thwarted, I decided to try my luck at Polly's. I paused at the edge of the Cassinis' driveway to watch Pete Graham play basketball.

It was nearing the last week of July, time slipping from my grasp. The heaviness of the summer air indicated that my entire world was about to change, quite possibly for the worst.

"Polly home?"

The ball slipped from his hands and rolled down the cement. He chased it, caught it, and then looked at me like I'd insulted him. "Huh?" he said.

"Polly?"

"She's riding bikes with some guy," Pete said, pausing to think. "Sorry, I forgot his name."

"Bruce?"

"That sounds right. You can wait if you want. But I don't know when they'll be back."

That's all Eve needed, to gaze out her window and see Bruce and Polly riding down the street. I watched Pete shoot free throws, watched his blond hair drip with sweat.

"Polly says you sell real estate. Do you like that?"

"I've got good connections, so the money is steady. Making more than I thought I would."

"That's why you do it? For money?" I was trying to figure out how one acquired an identity. Mine wasn't working out too well.

"Got to pay the bills," he said.

"Well, I know, but . . . is it what you always wanted to do? It's who you are?"

"It's what I do, not who I am."

"They're not the same thing?"

"They don't have to be, no."

"People are nice to me because I play tennis, not because I'm me," I said, remembering Pete's sudden friendliness—*after* he knew I was an athlete.

150

"That's not true."

"You'd be surprised how true that is," I said. It wasn't a feeling, it was a fact.

He attempted a layup, missing. He seemed tired of talking, or of me. I took this as my cue to leave. As I started up the hill he called to me, "Hey, Hall?"

I turned. "Hmmm?"

"I'm agenting a house for the sportscaster guy from Channel Five news. You should set up a profile of yourself for a news segment. They do stuff like that on that channel—local athletes."

I nodded. "I'll talk to my coach about it," I said, lying. "See what he says." That's all I needed, having my crappy game broadcast to the city. "You'll tell Polly I stopped by?"

"OK. See you," he said.

I pushed my bike up the hill, passing Eve's house with a pit in my stomach.

Luke, out of nowhere, pulled up and bumped the front wheel of his bike into mine, giving me a jolt. What a long, boring week it had been without his good-looking face. He was tanned and fresh-looking. "Hey," he said. "You're home? From your tournament?"

"As of last night."

"D'you win?"

"Uh-huh."

"I called you. Did you get my messages?" he asked.

"I did. But we had to leave before six-thirty in the morning. By the time the day's matches were over and we ate dinner in Denver I didn't get back until nine-thirty or so every night. I was too tired to call you, sorry."

"That's OK. I figured as much," he said. "I was on my way to Polly's. Thought you'd be there."

"She's around here somewhere with Bruce," I said.

"Want to go to 7-Eleven?"

I nodded. We pushed our bikes side by side up the street. I figured I'd talk about Luke's problems instead of my own. I needed to get away from them. "So what did you decide to do about the chess team?"

"Huh?"

"The chess team. You know, are you going to join it again? Tell Bruce to mind his business?"

"Well, probably not. The trips to other schools for the meets weren't fun, anyway."

I was confused. "But you weren't just on the team. You were the captain. You liked it. If you explained to Bruce why you like it, he'd understand. I know he would."

Luke shrugged and ran his fingers through his hair. "Some of those trophies were cheap, anyway."

"But it's not about the *trophies,*" I said, exasperated. "It's about the hard work you put into it—you know, accomplishing something."

He looked at me sort of funny. "It wasn't that hard, Holloway, I was just good at it."

My guts churned for some reason. "So that's it? You're done?"

He stopped walking altogether and thought about it. "I'm not trying to be an ass or anything, but why do you care?"

"But in the pool it sounded like you—"

"I guess I was thinking out loud in the pool. You're the only person I know who has trophies, so you know about things like that."

His reasoning shook me. This was glorious reasoning if ever there was. Why didn't my brain work this way? One small conversation in a pool and that was the extent of his torment? It was solved now? How? Nothing was actually resolved. He won trophies. Succumbed to peer pressure. Quit the chess team. And so now it was all better? Where was the dilemma? The anguish? The agony? I expected bitterness and confusion and pain!

What a glorious, stupendous, guiltless brain Luke possessed.

"Hey, Holloway?"

"Huh?"

"This is your house. We're here," Luke said.

"Oh," I said in a haze, "so we are."

A neighbor's dog barked through a fence, welcoming me back to reality.

"Let me run inside, grab some cash," I said. "Take me three seconds."

"I'll park my bike," he said. "Let's walk."

"Sure. Be back in a sec."

The news of Luke Kimberlin spread like wildfire among my brothers and the Choirboys. I was interrogated earlier by the Choirboy panel and found them half impressed and half hostile. Apparently, Luke's older sister wasn't just a pretty face, she was a goddess. And she had something that my brothers and the Choirboys did not— a driver's license and a cherry-red BMW with a license plate that read STAYSEE.

I maintained a slice of sympathy for them. A license was a big deal; none of them could drive. A few had permits but no one owned a car. Still, I had no real interest in Michael's quest for Stacey. I had enough of my own problems.

I crept inside to gather some money. The Choirboys looked me over like it was *their* house and I was the intruder. Dressed in tae kwon do outfits, they resembled the Pillsbury Doughboy. They loitered in our kitchen, waiting for my mom to drive them to some stupid martial arts exhibition or something.

Michael said, "Who's outside?"

"No one."

"Is that Luke Kimberlin?"

"No."

"Yes it is. Find out if Stacey has a boyfriend."

"She does. He's a freshman in college. Luke told me."

"But Stacey is only seventeen!"

Michael cornered me at the dining room table. I was about to crush his summer romance plans. As if Stacey Kimberlin would even *consider* dating a Pillsbury Doughboy.

"I'm only telling you what Luke told me," I said, freeing myself from all responsibility.

"If she has a boyfriend, why is she always at the movies with her girlfriends?"

"What am I, a mind reader?"

"Can you find it in your heart to get off your princess ass and get some information?"

"No, I cannot get off my princess ass and do anything, not when you ask like that."

Luke called, "Holloway!" through the screen door.

The Choirboys slipped further into disarray. They

continued observing me as if I was under glass. "I don't believe," Michael said, "that Hall is hanging out with a Kimberlin and I'm stuck here with you farts."

That short, sweet conversation gave me something that for all of my thirteen years I was unable to get for myself: a look of respect from Michael and the surge of power I felt as a result. I shoved a few meager dollar bills into my pocket and smiled. Once I walked out the door, my brothers' opinions had no claim on me. I was a free woman.

"Cut through the park?" Luke asked.

"Sure."

We trampled through park grasses and then fragrant weeds, stunned by pollen, 7-Eleven in our sights. I felt kind of happy for a moment, still contemplating the workings of Luke Kimberlin's brain.

In the 7-Eleven parking lot vehicles sped and weaved. We dodged two cars but didn't see the third. The car lunged.

"Holloway!"

"Agg!"

"Look out!" Luke pulled me back, hard.

I let out a yelp.

Brakes slammed. Tires screeched.

My legs quivered at the notion of sudden, painful death. I couldn't catch my breath. "Crap."

"Are you OK, Holloway?"

The car was a centimeter from my left knee. Would've broken it for sure. Blood pounded through my veins, making me light-headed.

"Holloway?"

Unable to move, we stood shocked and motionless in front of the car. A large man occupied the driver's seat. Next to him sat a striking redhead, all teeth and big lips. "You damn kids. Running out in front of cars. Get on the sidewalk!"

Luke grabbed my shoulder firmly. "Are you OK?"

I could barely speak. I looked down, making sure my kneecap was still attached to my leg. "I don't know . . ."

Resting his hand on the hood of the car, Luke bent down toward my knee. "It's nicked."

The man punched the horn. "Get out of the way! Damn idiot kids!"

Luke raised his hand, stone-faced, and flipped him off. Just like that. Courting danger. It was amazing. Beautiful, even. The guy struggled to unbuckle his seat belt to come after us, I guess. The woman yelled at her companion, shoving him in disapproval. Luke stood serene, waiting to see what would happen. I wasn't sure whether to cry, run, or—in the spirit of Eve—pee in my pants.

"Come on, Luke." I pulled at his sleeve.

"Wait a minute."

"Come on."

Luke obliged and we slid out of harm's way. The car sped off. He looked at me. "Do you need to sit down?"

"I can't believe you gave that guy the finger," I said.

"He wasn't going to do anything. It was his fault. We had the right of way. He nearly killed you."

My knee. Almost broken.

Death is preferable to a busted knee. A broken knee would sideline me for six months. Coach would go nuts. Berserk. Damaged flesh. Useless talent. Coach betrayed. Berserk Coach. Delirious Coach. Wouldn't be pretty. It'd be a rampage. Nostrils would flare. *Hit by a car? A sitting duck. Unbelievable! Trying to give a man a heart attack or what?*

Have to be careful. My body is not my own. I shouldn't even leave the house. Go nowhere. Go to the court. Then home. Play tennis and stay home. Knees are safe at home. Do not have a life. Do not live. Play tennis and go home. Tennis for a life. Breathe it, eat it, sleep it. No life. To the court and home. Need nothing. Be nothing. Want nothing. Love nothing. *Stay home.*

"An inch more and you'd be toast."

He put his hand on my back. I thought about the blank head of Luke Kimberlin. It pacified me.

Other people had needs they guarded as best they could to protect themselves. I *needed* to not be sent to Bickford, to not have everyone find out I suddenly sucked at tennis. Melissa *needed* our friendship enough to suffer occasional disrespect. My brothers *needed* to pick on me so they wouldn't feel bad about not being tennis champions. Where need filled the souls of others, Luke was hollow. His so-called chess dilemma, which was no dilemma at all, proved it. He needed nothing, his guts *ached* for nothing. He couldn't be hurt. He was free to flip someone off and not care about the consequences.

More than anything else, more than his good looks or his confidence, it was this lack of need, lack of anguish that I suddenly wished was mine. His head was perfectly blank. Perfection rested in blank heads. Oh, the tennis I could play with the empty head of Luke Kimberlin!

I grabbed his hand, hoping his empty head was contagious so I could be mean, strong, and free. If only I could switch our brains, I could forget about Janie going crazy on that court, forget that maybe I was going crazy, too, forget that Coach's voice wasn't in my head and play tennis, *freely.*

Air-conditioning turned my sweat to ice as the door

to the 7-Eleven shut, enclosing us inside. I stood at the front counter, making sure my knee was able to bend, and watched Luke in the candy aisle. He chose a Kit Kat and ever so quickly shoved it in his pocket, stealing it as if he was entitled. As always, anything could happen when with Luke. And something was happening. It just wasn't good.

My heart sparked at the danger. Cringed at the deceit. And I knew right then that I'd never possess the blank head of Luke Kimberlin. Suddenly my own head felt too full to even ask him why, why, why he would do such a thing.

• Chapter Fourteen •

I babysit for my next-door neighbors, the Jordans, when the sitter they trust isn't available. I'm not their first choice; they call me out of desperation. My mom says it will make me responsible. So far it's only made me annoyed.

The Jordans have one child. He's got pale eyes and a crew cut. He can't say *h,* so he calls me Wall instead of Hall. Mrs. Jordan is anal about teeth brushing; she reminds me a zillion times to have the kid brush his teeth. I never do. Ever. I figure they need a break. It's a wonder he has any teeth left with all that brushing.

The Jordans' house smells like Ajax. And it's *clean:* never any dust, dirt, or dirty dishes in the sink. Mr. Jordan escapes the smell of Ajax by spending time in the garage. Wearing grubby clothes, he pounds nails into wood for some mystery project that's never completed. I'd pound nails into wood, too, if I had to live with Mrs. Jordan. She has that effect on people.

Regardless of the circumstances, being at the Jordans' gave me a quiet place to do my "homework assignment." As punishment for my botched win at the Cherry Creek Invitational (I still can't believe he thought I was trying to humiliate that girl), Coach "suggested" I write a report on sportsmanship. For inspiration, he gave me a DVD of his favorite match, the 2001 U.S. Open quarterfinal match between Pete Sampras and Andre Agassi.

Neither player breaks serve. They go four hard sets and every set ends in a tiebreaker. The crowd is manic with joy. Andre and Pete are so focused they're not human anymore. They are tennis gods. They both defy pain *and* inhabit it. I can barely sit still watching.

Pain like this is what Trent calls sportsmanship. Suffering *justifies* the victory. Watching them play to win, no matter the cost, is supposed to make me ashamed of myself or something.

Once when pro player Kim Clijsters delivered an acceptance speech for a Grand Slam runner-up trophy, she gave it in Flemish, French, and English. I wondered suddenly if she had a voice inside her head that made her win. And if so, which language did it speak?

I thought briefly about Roger Federer, wondering how long he'd had to lose before he started to win. A week? A month? A year? Thinking about it made my head hurt.

Sportsmanship is about trying your best. Pure shots are the goal. Arrogance has no place in competitive sports, I wrote.

The doorbell went ballistic. *Ding-dong, ding-dong.*

Polly and Melissa stood on the Jordans' front step, their faces mashed into the screen.

"Hall, answer the door already," Polly said.

"Let us in," Melissa said.

"Hey! What are you doing?" I was suddenly flattered I had such great friends.

"Your brother said you were here," Polly said.

I unlocked the screen door. "Be quiet. The kid's asleep."

Melissa entered wearing a yellow shirt and green shorts—a fashion nightmare.

"What's that smell?" she asked.

"Ajax. What are you guys doing?"

"Hanging out. How late will you be here?"

"Nine-thirty."

"Too bad," Polly said. "Who are those people at your house?"

"It really reeks in here," Melissa said.

"I know. What people?"

Polly noted the cleanliness and rested her gaze on the Agassi match. "Don't know. That's why I'm asking."

Melissa continued to complain. "Can't you open a window or something?"

"Was it Coach? You'd recognize him—big man with a shaved head?"

"I didn't see anyone, just heard the noise. Your mom was laughing. Anyway, Bruce said he can get us passes to the country club on Friday. You and me and Luke can go together." She looked at Melissa. "Sorry, Meiissa."

Melissa shrugged. "I don't mind."

"Oh, you and Bruce are quite the item now," I said.

"We kissed," Polly declared, waiting for me to explode in approval.

"And how was that?" I asked.

"Slobbery," she said, cracking up. "Like kissing a dog."

I laughed, wondering if she had worn her orange lip gloss for that kiss. If she had, Bruce was probably still wiping it off his face. "Spend a lot of time kissing your dog, do you?"

"Gross!" Polly said.

"Bruce might be mad if he thinks a dog kisses better than him."

Polly shrugged, gleeful. "At least Bruce doesn't have doggy breath."

"Can we go outside?" Melissa said. "The smell is making me dizzy."

"It's not that bad," Polly said.

We stepped outside and sat in the grass to cleanse our noses from Ajax. Mrs. Jordan would have a coronary if she knew Polly and Melissa were over. I'd been told many times that I wasn't allowed to consort with friends while on duty. Friends and dirty teeth were major causes for alarm with Mrs. Jordan.

"Ahh," said Melissa. "Much better."

"What's wrong with Eve, anyway?" Polly asked. "I called her to see if she wanted to walk up here with us and she hung up on me."

I didn't want to explain Eve's mood swings. "I don't know what's up with Eve," I lied.

Polly glanced at the dimming skies. "It's getting late. Gotta be home before dark. Don't forget about the country club. I'll give you the details later," she said, as they walked backward across the Jordans' lawn.

*　　*　　*

Indeed, Coach was at my house, along with Annie, when I got home. The sound of forks scraping on plates filled the dining room. All eyes were on me as I entered. Identical smiles plastered on their faces. It couldn't be good news.

"Hall, have some cake?" my mom asked.

"What kind is it?"

"The congratulations kind. Annie brought it over."

"Hi, Chickadee," Annie said.

"Congratulations for what?"

"Bickford Tennis Academy sent you two plane tickets, round-trip, first-class, to come and view their operation," Coach bellowed, beating my dad to the punch.

I said something profound, like, "Huh?"

"Poor girl," my dad said, "she's in shock. Look at that face."

The four of them burst into a fit of laughter so loud that their jolly, gut-busting chuckles of glee echoed in my head, shaking my very brains.

"How?" I asked.

"Thomas Fountain helped me arrange it," Trent said. "They're anxious to meet you. I faxed them a list of the tournaments you've won. You're quite a catch, you know."

"But it's so much money. Why would they send for

me if they know I can't afford it? What, did you lie to them?"

"Of course not," my mom scoffed. "We're not going to worry about the money right now. We're going to look around, see if it's a nice place."

I didn't want to be anywhere *near* the academy. "A nice place?" I said. "Look around?"

Again, they burst into torrid laughter. Trent's low bleats bellowed forth and were absorbed into the walls and carpet equally. Hee-hees saturated the room. I felt queasy and grabbed hold of the counter to keep my balance.

Annie shook my shoulder. "It's so exciting, Hall!"

Annie, my beloved Annie, who normally had zero interest in my chosen game of tennis, had been sucked over to the other side, to the ruin-Hall's-life side. Suddenly Annie's present of the Swiss flag seemed more like a diversion tactic than an actual gift.

While I stared at my Swiss flag every night, smitten with the beauty of Roger Federer, they'd contacted Bickford Academy—spoken *about* me in *regard* to tennis. Stupid flag. Annie had bribed me further into doom by appealing to my lust for Roger Federer's gliding passing shots. I can't believe I fell for it.

"When?" I asked. "When are we going?"

"In three days. Saturday morning. First of August," my mom said as she handed me a piece of betrayal cake.

"A good sign, first of August," Trent said.

"Great," I said. "First of August. Terrific."

Hope filled my mom's face. "We're so proud, Hall."

The hope on my mother's face, ugh, the hope. The expectation she doesn't dare voice. Wants to protect me from the expectation, not be the cause of it. But it's there. Expectation. The hope that all this is for something bigger than me, her, this family, this city, this country, and this world. My God, the hope on my mother's face. The hope that I will succeed. It covers her like maple syrup. My game, so unrefined: it is unworthy of that hope.

• Chapter Fifteen •

Lively jabber filled Stacey's car. "I'm freaking out . . . Driving around . . . We're already an hour late . . . The car runs out of gas . . . My cell phone's battery is dead . . . Have to walk . . ."

BMWs really are driving machines, just like the ad claims. They corner well. Travel at top speed. I wouldn't have known we were doing fifty in a twenty-five-mile-an-hour zone had I not been looking at the speedometer. Stacey Kimberlin, goddess, sister of Luke, was the worst driver ever. She would need that pretty face of hers to thwart many traffic tickets. Already she'd cut off two drivers and didn't even say whoops.

Stacey was chirpy. Spastic. All sorts of cutesy tales

were flying out of her mouth. The girl was a Rolodex of unimportant stories. Occasionally I've wished I was as dumb as a chirpy girl like Stacey, but I'm not. I rarely rattle off cute stories to people I don't know.

". . . I go to the gas station for help, and there's *Brandon*!" she said, as if we cared.

Luke glanced at me, rolling his eyes at Stacey's tirade. Bruce sighed heavily, looking out the window. Polly and I got the giggles.

Oblivious, Stacey stared at me from the rearview mirror. "I know your brothers," she said. "Mark and Ben, right?"

I bit my tongue. "Michael and Brad."

"That's right," she said as she sped through a yellow light. She possessed the same flawless forehead as Luke.

"They're in love with you," I said.

"Isn't that sweet. How cute!" She was already turning my comment into some bit of whimsy to tell her friends. I was sorry I'd said anything.

"Yes, it's very cute," I said. "Adorable."

We survived the car ride, barely, and ventured into the splendor of the country club. I was here as an actual guest—experiencing the club as one of the pretend wealthy instead of by the sweat of my brow and near-great backhand. My stomach churned. I wasn't supposed to be having fun; I was supposed to be packing for Florida.

"Gotta put my sportsmanship essay in Coach's office first," I said.

"Lead the way," Luke said.

The club delighted Polly. Her body sort of unfolded, taking everything in, eyes wide. "Ooh. You get to come here every day," she said.

"I'm here for work, not enjoyment. It's not the same thing." If she only knew. Coach had already called me at home and warned me not to be late for practice later on today, *and* not to bring spectators. "Last practice before going to Bickford, Hall," he'd warned. "Better be prepared to play. We're going through every shot you've got," he'd said.

"I figured as much," I'd said.

"And by the way, I'll be visiting Janie again when you get back. You're coming with me. You can't ignore her, Hall. It'll be good for you to see her."

I was going with him?

I held the phone, unable to answer him. Thoughts of Janie rattling me.

We filed into Coach's spacious office. Polly gazed out his windows, which overlooked the golf course. I was glad that Coach was on court, teaching club women the basics. He wouldn't have wanted everyone here. Bruce

171

tapped a large glass jar filled with quarters, nickels, and dimes—Trent hated the jingle of change in his pockets. I often raided the jar to buy myself Diet Cokes while waiting for a ride home.

"Whoa, look at this!" Luke said, gazing in awe at the baseball on Trent's desk. Bruce rushed over, both of them smothering the ball with hot breath and greedy hands.

"You're not supposed to pick it up," I said.

"What is it?" Polly asked.

"It's a Roger—"

"It's a Roger Maris baseball," Luke said. "Roger Maris! The real thing. Look how old it is!"

"Please don't pick it up. Trent'll freak."

"Put it down, Luke," Bruce said.

"Make me," Luke spat.

The ball was protected by a plastic case; he wasn't going to hurt it, really. But Coach didn't like people touching his baseball. It was an authentic signed ball. People had offered to buy it, but Trent never even considered it. He liked it in his office, where they could be jealous.

"It's old," said Polly.

"That's the point. This is Roger Maris's *signature*!" Luke said.

"So?" Polly said. I could sympathize with her lack of enthusiasm. I rarely understood the stupid stuff guys got excited about, either.

Bruce looked at her, disappointed. "He's a legend, Polly. He's dead now. He played for the Yankees."

"Luke, quit picking it up. I'm serious," I said.

"I'm not hurting it."

"Coach will be mad if he sees fingerprints on the case, though."

Begrudgingly, he lowered it back down.

I tossed my sportsmanship essay on Trent's desk and turned to my followers. I was happy: for once I didn't have to eat lunch alone. "Let's eat first. I'm starved."

Polly clucked her tongue like a duck, agreeing.

We clomped down the stairs, toward the snack bar. When Luke suggested we all meet tonight at his neighbors' house to swim, Polly kicked me so hard I was certain my shin was bloodied. She'd been highly jealous when I told her about sneaking into the pool house—I'd embellished the details, since the girl was dramatic and always expected firecrackers.

"I don't know which house. Bruce, meet me halfway? And you can show me?" Polly said.

"Sure, halfway. At ten," Bruce said.

"At ten," everyone agreed.

We swam after lunch. Polly and I fiddled around in the shallow end, trying not to get our hair wet.

"Dodgeball!" Luke screamed, smacking Bruce in the face with a ball. "Two points!"

Stunned by the blow, Bruce fell beneath the water's surface, not moving.

"Did you see that?" Polly asked. "That had to hurt."

"Is he conscious?"

The water moved gently, with no Bruce in sight.

"He isn't moving," Polly said, voice low.

"Luke! You better help him!" I yelled.

"Luke," Polly pleaded.

Luke took tentative steps toward Bruce, closer, closer . . . The water trembled, and Bruce sprang forth, red-faced, ball in hand, and launched it into Luke's neck with all his might. *Thunk!*

"Two points," Bruce hollered.

Polly looked at me with disgust. "How clever."

I scooped the chlorinated water onto my arms. "Wish I were that easily entertained."

She held out her arm for me to inspect. "Do I look burned?"

"A little pink, maybe. It'll be gone by tomorrow."

"Did I tell you Maren loves Bruce?"

"Why, what's the big deal?"

"Westland Prep is one of the top private schools in America. Did you know over sixty percent of their graduates go on to Ivy League universities? Their math department is *intense.*"

"Luke says it's pretty tough," I agreed.

"I'm just saying that's why Maren likes him—Bruce is academically inclined." She glanced at the water bobbing around her. "I wonder what that would be like, going to Westland," she said, deep in thought. "I wonder what it takes to get in."

"Are you joking? You've whined about math camp all summer. Polly, you need more math homework like you need a hole in your head," I said.

"I guess," she said.

"Holloway, do you guys want to play?" Luke called, holding up the ball coyly.

"No thanks."

"We won't hit you in the face, promise. I'll spot you ten points?"

"No thanks."

Luke shrugged and thrust the ball into Bruce's gut. "Two points!"

Polly pulled her hair up in a makeshift ponytail and just as quickly let it drop back down. That small movement made me gasp. Hair in a makeshift ponytail and then back down—I'd seen Janie do that maybe a hundred times on court. Exactly like that. Ponytail up, then down. On court. Her face showing the stress of the game. Her maniac father screaming. Me watching her play. Me watching her father scream. Hair in a ponytail, then down. Just like that.

Me watching her fall to the court. Lost. Gone. Mind gone . . . to where? Where had Janie's mind gone? Where was my mind going? Was I Janie? Drop to the court and she was gone. Drop to the court and have no mind. Not a blank head. Not perfection. But no head. A *headless* Janie on that court.

Janie sent Polly here, to me. Not an angel to comfort me. Polly was no angel. She was a ghost. Here to torment me. Pouty cheeks. No comfort for me in those cheeks. Only pain. Agony. Defeat.

Polly was here to tell me I'd be defeated on the courts of Bickford tomorrow. Drop to the court, mind gone. Like headless Janie. Polly was a ghost. She was not real.

I rocked in the water, trying to slow my reeling brain. Trying to run from Janie, wherever she was. In a straitjacket somewhere. Babbling incoherently. On a court. Me watching.

I moved my hands through the cool water. It sloshed upward, dotting my face with single wet droplets.

"What's the matter, Hall?" Polly asked.

Was she Polly or a ghost?

"Nothing's the matter," I said. *Breathe in. Breathe out.* Stop thinking. Get a blank head. Polly doesn't even know Janie. Janie didn't send her. Doesn't even know her. *Breathe in. Breathe out.*

"You look like you're going to throw up," Polly said.

Fingers splayed, I separated the water with slow swoops, wishing I was Moses and it was the Red Sea. *Swoop, swoop.* I didn't have the power of Moses, though, and my sea of Janie and expectations flooded me. "I'm OK," I said. "I'm OK."

Bruce caught Polly's attention. She smiled big as he jumped wildly off the diving board. I let the waves I created lull me, cleanse me. Drain my thoughts.

"Have you ever peed in a pool?" Polly said absently, still watching Bruce.

I exhaled and then laughed.

"When I was little I used to pee in the pool all the time—too cold to get out. There's all that water there anyway," she explained.

I sent a wave of water toward her, forcing a hollow smile onto my face. "Me too," I said. "Me too."

• Chapter Sixteen •

It was five after ten. I sat in the pitch-darkness of my back deck, on a lawn chair. The night air was soggy, windy. Smelled of rain. I was supposed to be in bed, asleep. And I was also supposed to be at Luke's neighbors' house, swimming with him, Bruce, and Polly. But I hadn't been able to force myself to go and called Luke, canceling. Seeing Polly morph into a ghost before my eyes still freaked me out. I couldn't face her again tonight. Besides, I didn't want to have to walk home sopping wet like I did the last time. I hadn't packed yet for Bickford. I didn't know what to pack besides my racquets.

The skies were moist. Specks of rain fell lightly onto

my face. I situated myself further into the chair cushion, with a big beach towel over my clothes for warmth.

The sky lit angrily. The backyard trees looked stark and timid in the harsh light. Like pretend trees. In a pretend yard.

I braced my feet on the deck planks.

Lightning struck the earth with deafening shrieks of thunder.

My shoulder blades bound tightly into knots as I looked up into the black night.

My hair was damp on top, dry underneath. I bit my lip, forcing my mind to be quiet. I wasn't sure what I feared more, heading to Bickford Tennis Academy in the morning or visiting Janie in a loony bin upon my return. Would Janie be in a straitjacket? Would she be able to speak? Would she hate me for playing tennis without her? Would she take one look at me and know I was a fraud?

The sky lit again. My house shrank in the brightness. It looked like a dollhouse, like a child's toy. I felt non-human here on the deck, a plaything, a tennis-playing action figure with a plastic racquet permanently glued into my plastic hand.

Thunder rolled evilly.

Raindrops started falling hard. They actually hurt as they made contact with my skin, tearing into my flesh like bullets. I tucked myself further into the towel. But I liked it that they hurt. That meant I could focus on the hurt, on the rain, and not on Janie. Or Bickford. Or that maybe I was turning into Janie.

I knew I'd forget about her the minute I stepped onto the Bickford courts. I always forgot about Janie when on a court—I was too busy trying to find Coach's voice in my head to think of Janie.

I suddenly felt insignificant. My life didn't feel real.

The back door creaked open. "Hall?" my mom called, stunned. "What are you doing up so late? And what are you doing *out here*? In the rain?"

"Needed some air."

"You better get to bed. The plane will leave without us. I hope you're all packed."

I nodded and lifted myself up off the chair.

"Get some sleep, honey," my mom said. "Big day tomorrow."

• Chapter Seventeen •

"**N**ot much further," the driver said. "A couple more miles. Come from Colorado, huh?"

Bickford Academy sent one of their lackeys to pick up my mom and me from the airport. I was stuck in the backseat while my mom rode shotgun. It was seven at night, and we had yet to eat dinner. The driver said one of the academy coaches planned on feeding us.

"Most of the kids here are from out of state, but you'll be our first from Colorado. This year we'll have twenty-five students from different countries, too," the driver said.

"How lovely," my mom said.

"The kids are divided by ages and skill levels."

"I imagine they'd have to be," my mom said.

"Of course, we aren't in full session right now. Official check-in doesn't happen until August twenty-seventh. I suppose you already know that from the literature we sent . . ."

I didn't know why this stupid man kept talking. Apparently he thought I was going to *attend* Bickford Academy. Not likely. I was only here so my mom, the Weak Link, could see how atrocious the place was. So far it wasn't working. Though I'd played tournaments in Florida before, Trent and Annie, not my mom, had acted as my chaperones. Now she took in each trivial sight like an excited tourist.

"Look at all the palm trees!" my mom squealed.

"Gee, a palm tree, neat," I said inaudibly.

"The atmosphere is so relaxing," she continued. "I feel a sudden urge for a banana daiquiri."

"I feel the urge for a barf bag."

"Did you say something, Hall?" the driver asked.

"The air feels swampy," I said. "Feel that? Muggy."

My mom shook her head. "It doesn't. It's nice."

"It's swampy."

"It's no such thing."

About thirty boys decked out in wrinkled white and navy Bickford Academy T-shirts ran down the middle of the street like a pack of rabid wolves. Each seemed to have a wealthy-looking forehead and tanned skin. Several of them could be considered downright gorgeous. The whole mess of them bobbed up and down on the pavement at various speeds, all staying within the group. Sweat flying. Sore muscles aching.

My mom watched me watch them. Our car and their jogging route met and went opposite directions. Soon another pack of wolves—girls in ponytails, with matching shirts and gray shorts—jogged past as well. An instructor yelled things at them to keep up morale. Exhaustion sat on the faces of some, pain on others. I expected as much.

"Evening conditioning run," the driver said.

"Doesn't *that* look fun," I said.

"Here we are. Beautiful, isn't it? You'll notice the entrance is secured. In case of escapes," he said, laughing.

The gatekeeper waved our car through.

"Escapes? Look how high those walls are!" I'd definitely need a ladder to flee.

"No one can leave without a pass," he said, reading my mind.

"Of course," my mom said, as if this was comforting.

The car slowed to five miles an hour for our viewing pleasure. Sprawling grounds prompted *oohs* and *aahs* from the front seat. It looked like a resort. I had hoped it would more or less resemble a prison or Marine Corps barracks. We drove along the perimeter of the compound.

"These three buildings are the boys' dorms; up farther are the girls'. The cafeteria, library, and staff offices are all housed in this main building. The pool is around back. Can you see from back there, Hall?"

"Yeah."

"We weren't expecting something so elaborate, were we, Hall?" my mom said.

"We have ten each of clay and grass courts and thirty-eight outside hard courts. Plus indoor hard courts as well."

"Hmmm."

"Our scheduling system is tight. The emphasis is on hard courts with adaptation techniques for clay and grass. You'll love clay," the driver said, looking at me from the rearview mirror, "it's great fun."

"I've won two tournaments on clay," I said.

One, two, three car doors slammed as we got out, inspecting the courts. My mom raised her eyebrows, trying to telepathically tell me this was great. I ignored her.

"Look at these courts. Not a nick in them!" she said.

"I'll let Phil know you're here," the driver said. "You must be starved. Nice meeting you both."

184

Whatever.

My mom could be impressed all she wanted. All she had to do was witness the grim, pasty-faced, unloved, exiled children, thousands of miles away from their hometowns, and the woman would break like fine china. Weak Link. I could hear her on the phone to my dad—*They're children, Frank* and *They look so sad*—and we'd be outta here.

I hadn't told any of my friends about my Bickford debacle, so my so-called secret was safe. The trip amounted to a few hours tonight and all day Sunday, with our plane leaving on Monday at 8:00 p.m. I figured I could handle anything, even Bickford, for thirty-one waking hours.

Phil was about forty, with a chin that was roughly the size of Nevada. He had simply huge dimples and a big, energetic voice.

"Hall Braxton!" he greeted me. "I'm Phil Flickett. I'm the head coach. You can call me Coach."

"No thanks. Trent is my coach."

Phil Flickett and his big chin were unfazed. "All right, call me Phil, then." He shook hands politely with my mom but continued to look at me as though I was an item, a commodity, a product.

"It's so wonderful of you to bring us here," my mom

gushed. "Hall's been working hard on her game. She's been with the same coach for years and years, so this is quite a new experience for us. Her coach is the one who contacted Thomas Fountain originally."

"Oh yes, Thomas is a friend of ours from way back. He scouts recruits for us now and then. Hall impressed him a great deal. But we'll talk tennis later. There's a good place to eat not far. How does ravioli sound?"

The veal-stuffed ravioli swam in a pool of red sauce. I chewed the rubbery pasta while I halfheartedly listened to my mom grill Phil and his big chin.

"What about the dorms? How are they set up?"

"There are three separate buildings for girls and three for boys. We call them villas. Each villa holds a different age group."

"The place seems cozy. Unusual for the size," my mom said, putty in the guy's hands.

"Glad you noticed. We're proud of that. Anyway, there are four girls to a room. Each villa also has four single rooms. The better girls in each age group get the singles."

I knew it—the *better girls* from each age group got the singles. It was unspoken although constant competition, even for a bedroom. My mom hated unnecessary competitiveness.

"I see," she said, her words breaking off in chunks.

Phil shoved garlic bread into his big dimpled cheeks, making him look like a chipmunk. Sensing my mother's disapproval, he tried calming it.

"We focus mainly on skills, coping under pressure, mental strategies. We don't turn out faceless robots. We stress individual style. No competing in every tournament that comes around, no need."

My mom exhaled and relaxed, significantly soothed. "Oh, that's nice."

"Yes, it's very nice," I said.

"It was a long flight," my mom said, as if I needed explaining. "It's a lot to grasp. Butterflies getting the best of her."

Butterflies, ha!

"Nah," Phil said. "She's a tough cookie. That delicate face doesn't fool me. We'll get you on a court tomorrow, get a stick in your hand, be good as new."

"Just butterflies," my mom said again.

"Your coach said you won the Junior Orange Bowl two years in a row?"

"Yes. I had easy draws."

"No such thing as an easy draw at the Junior Orange Bowl," Phil the Chin said. "That's a huge accomplishment."

"It is," my mom agreed.

"It *was* an easy draw," I protested. "Two players in my half defaulted."

"She got to the finals of the Copper Bowl and did well at the Columbus Indoors in Ohio as well. Won the Great Pumpkin Sectionals."

Stunned, I looked at my mom. The woman had barely uttered a tennis term in her entire life, and she was choosing to become an expert now?

"Haven't played many tournaments this summer. Why?"

The only tournament I'd played was the Cherry Creek Invitational, thank God. I'd made such a mess of it, I felt sick just thinking about it. If I didn't start playing some tournaments, my ranking was going to plummet. In fact it probably already had. "Coach says the competition isn't hard enough. Wants me to concentrate on drills instead," I said.

"Is that why you didn't play in the USTA Girls 14's National Clay Court Championship in July?"

I shrugged. It fit that he kept mentioning the Junior Orange Bowl and the National Clay Courts; they were Florida events.

"But you won the Clay Courts last year; you didn't want to defend your title?" he asked, prodding further.

Trent withdrew me from the Clay Courts after Janie had her breakdown. He didn't want to push me, I think.

But I didn't want to explain that to The Chin. My mom recognized me floundering and piped up.

"Money is a factor," she said, rescuing me. "All the traveling gets to be quite a financial burden."

Phil nodded. "If you stay visible, stay winning, you can get some sponsorship deals going. Nike, Reebok, Fila . . . get free equipment at the very least."

"Representatives from those companies have already contacted her. Her coach doesn't like the idea."

"Why?" The Chin asked me.

"Because I'm not for sale."

"Oh," he said.

"Her coach feels it's important to change her equipment as her game grows. He doesn't want her feeling forced to use specific brands. Prince ships her free racquets every so often. Right now we're more concerned with the cost of coaching, not equipment."

"I see," The Chin said. That shut him up for a while. But not nearly long enough. "Have you played any international tournaments yet?"

"Only one in Mexico, in February, a lowly level 5 tournament. I lost in the first round to a girl from Argentina," I said.

"That girl was *eighteen*," my mom added.

I gulped down my Diet Coke until only ice remained and looked around, hoping to spot our absent waiter.

"Thomas Fountain was impressed with your serve-and-volley game. What's your best shot otherwise?"

I couldn't bring myself to answer. The level of his coaching prowess was questionable. A good coach is supposed to *see* a player's game, not *ask*.

"Just butterflies," my mom assured The Chin.

I opted for the indoor hard courts at noon on Sunday. I hadn't had a racquet in my palm in a day and a half. My hand actually itched for it—felt complete again. The Weak Link sat to the side and watched me hit ground strokes against the backboard. Her face was fresh, spry, and curious. I ignored her. Phil joined her with cups of hot coffee.

A group of girls goofed off, waiting to watch.

"Katie!" The Chin called. "Rally with Hall?"

"Sure," she hollered, stepping on court. I'm pretty tall, but Katie towered over me by four inches. We hit easy shots so she could warm up. "I'm Katie."

She didn't look quite as depraved as I'd expected.

"I'm Hall. You thirteen?"

"Fourteen. Been here two years. Did I see you at early admission?"

"No. I'm just here for the weekend. I won't be back."

"Too bad." She caught the ball. "Ready?"

"Let's do it."

She let me serve first. The ball echoed slightly in the building's steely acoustics. The twang made my heart skip.

Thump . . . thump . . .

. . . thump . . . thump . . .

Katie was a baseliner. Although she was a year older, her skills were years behind mine. Her strokes were haphazard and soft. If Trent were here, he'd holler at her lack of effort.

Thump . . . thump . . .

. . . thump . . . thump . . .

I charged the net like a warrior, suffocating her intentions.

. . . thump . . . Out!

Katie's next shot barreled down the court. I met it before it hit the ground, tenderly lifting my racquet. Hit gently, easy like an egg. Barely clearing the net, it rolled as it landed on her side of the court. A flawless drop shot.

I felt like kissing that ball.

"Vicious drop shot, Hall! Looking good! Exact amount of ease," Phil said, confirming.

I won the next three games. Katie made a good-natured grimace. The girl wasn't the least bit depraved for someone who'd done two years at Bickford.

"I shoulda known you were a serve-and-volley girl," she said. "Most of us are baseliners."

"That's good for now, Katie," Phil called. "Send Millicent over."

Katie walked to the net, waiting to shake my hand. It seemed silly since we hadn't played a whole set, but I obliged. I thought briefly of Trent and sportsmanship.

I was relaxed, my head clear. I was playing like my old self again. Power and finesse dominated my strokes. Maybe the whole fiasco at the Cherry Creek Invitational was just an off week. I'd been worried about nothing. Trent's voice was gone, but apparently I didn't need it here. I was a fine player without his voice. A warrior after all.

Katie lowered her voice. "Millicent Mumfred is sixteen—turning pro this year, in time for the Aussie Open. She's good—high-world-ranking good. Good enough to have a single room. They tell you about the single rooms?"

"Yes."

Katie looked around. "Millicent hates sprinting to the net. If I were you, I'd hit a few more drop shots," she said.

"Really? Shame on you, giving me pointers."

She shrugged. "It's only fair. Millicent's been sizing you up since you stepped on court."

The Chin hollered, "Any day now, Katie!"

"See you," she said, and then called, "Millicent, you're up!"

"Hall, need a drink?" my mom called nervously.

"No."

Millicent Mumfred, a big healthy girl, walked to the net. We shook hands. Bickford Tennis Academy was high on manners, of that I was certain. The complete absence of grim, pale-faced girls concerned me.

"Hello, Hall," she mumbled, indifferent to me, my game, and the fact that I existed. "I hope you're ready to lose."

I ignored her silly head games. "Need to warm up?"

"Not for a scrawny thirteen-year-old." Tossing her hair, she waddled like a duck to the baseline. No wonder she didn't like drop shots—her butt was obviously too big to get to them.

The group of kids watching respectfully off court had increased by ten, including Katie. Reverence so dominated the air I felt like I was in church.

Thump . . . thump . . . thump . . .

. . . thump . . . thump . . . thump . . .

Millicent was better than she looked, even with the big butt. She tried rushing me: she bounced the ball exactly once before she tossed it, hurtling it at me. I'd barely look up from the end of one point to find her in mid-toss again, serving as fast as she could to throw off my rhythm. She wasn't so much a great strategist as she was a Sherman tank.

. . . *thump* . . . *thump* . . . *thump* . . .

She hit a passing shot wide. "Out," I called.

"That was in," she said. "I could see it from here."

"Wasn't. Out."

"It was in," The Chin called from the bleachers, taking her side. No way did he see that point. He kept his eyes on me to see what I'd do. What an amateur. Takes more than a bad call to shake me, stupid man.

"Fine, in. Your game. My serve."

Thump . . . *thump* . . . *thump* . . . Her point.

Thump . . . *thump* . . . *thump* . . . Her point.

Thump . . . *thump* . . . *thump* . . . My point.

Her point, her point. Her game.

"Shit," I said under my breath. *Get it together. Win!*

Millicent Mumfred twirled her racquet as though it was a baton and she was in a Main Street parade.

Thump . . . *thump* . . .

. . . *thump* . . . *thump* . . .

What to do? What to do? My brain was mush. In my junior career I'd learned a catalog of ways to win points, games, matches. Though I'd recited them aloud this morning, I couldn't conjure up one successful shot. The flogging I'd experienced at Cherry Creek was happening again. What type of player was I without Trent's advice? Should I . . .

Stay at the baseline?

Hit a passing shot?

Try a lob? Nothing. I was helpless.

Win, dammit, I told myself. *Win!*

"Pick up the pace, Hall, or she'll have you running all over the court. Stop play," The Chin said as the ball went wide. "Hall?"

"Yes?"

"Don't let her control the point. You're rushing the stroke. Run around the ball until you get the racquet in a decent hitting position. Pick up some speed."

"OK."

My mom, an encouraging but semi-removed (until lately, that is) tennis parent, looked as though she would throw up, this man telling me what to do and all. She'd never heard Trent threaten to make me run sprints before, obviously. She nodded wildly at me from the bleachers, the hope on her face making me ill.

"Patience," The Chin repeated. "Rush your foot speed, not the stroke."

"I understand."

On the next four points I let the balls pass me, ran them down, and slammed them in one fluid motion at her forehand. "Agg!"

. . . *thump* . . .

"Crap."

I got one of the four.

"Great!" The Chin said, voice energetic. "That's it! You've almost got it!"

Almost got it? Was the man insane? I only got *one*! I was nearly crying.

Thump . . . *thump* . . . *thump* . . .

"OK, ladies, that's good for now."

Taking his cue, Millicent let my return fly by as she walked to the net, waiting for me. "You suck," she said, without eye contact, as I approached.

I couldn't think of a thing to say.

I traipsed over to my spectators. I swallowed to keep myself from crying. "Did you see that? Holy hell, did you see that? She clobbered me!" I screamed The Chin. "I wanted to win. Shit!"

"Hall!" my mom said, turning pink. The use of bad language could *send* my mother. I didn't care. Not only had I lost, but now I was throwing a tantrum. Nothing made sense. Why, why, why couldn't I hit that damn ball? The Weak Link and The Chin stared at me, dumbfounded.

"Did you *see* that?" I repeated. "She *clobbered* me."

Phil held his big chin in his hand, covering the dimples. "I didn't expect you to give Millicent much trouble. She's three years older. Been at the academy three years."

"How did she do that?" I demanded.

Phil looked like he was in deep thought, chin still cupped in his hand. "You've had some substantial coaching, Hall," he said finally. "Bickford can do better. Too bad I didn't have the radar out, but some of those serves were . . . The net coverage you've got, that's some awesome net coverage at thirteen."

The man was obviously a fool. "What game were you watching?" I said sarcastically.

"Hall!" my mom said.

"Didn't you see all my errors?"

"Hall!" Again, my mom.

"If you thought that was good, you must be blind."

"But the pace you're able to generate is awesome—"

"I played like shit! I hate this game!"

"Holloway Louise Braxton!"

Abrupt silence covered the court.

I gulped water. I couldn't've cared less. People were worried about politeness, not realizing I was *losing my mind* right along with my tennis skills.

Strangely, the corners of The Chin's mouth turned upward ever so slightly. He seemed pleased—at what, I'd no idea. Like I said, he was a fool.

It was a farce. Who was I kidding? Tennis didn't love me anymore. Dead Grandpa Bonus Fund or not, regal surroundings like Bickford belonged to girls who possessed voices of tennis wisdom in their heads, instead of the rocks I had in mine.

• Chapter Eighteen •

My mom went with The Chin to look at the nearby private school the academy kids attended. I skipped out on the festivities under the pretense of touring the dorm rooms, like I cared. Katie and I sat in her room sharing a bag of potato chips.

She flung an official academy T-shirt toward me. "You can have it—I've got a million. It's a little faded, but the new ones have that funky smell from the screen printing—takes, like, a year before that smell leaves."

"A souvenir. Thanks." I didn't want it but decided to be low-key. I wasn't here to pick a fight or anything. She was right about the funky smell from the logo ink. The Chin had lent my mom a Bickford sweatshirt that smelled like Pepto-Bismol. "The other day I saw two huge groups of kids running. D'you run every day?"

Katie looked at me like I was stupid. "Well, yeah. Twice a day. In the morning before breakfast—that's the worst—and later, after matches and drills."

"I hate running."

"Who doesn't? It's pointless. Easier in a group, though. Better than doing it alone."

"How long have you been here again?" I asked.

"Two years. I'm from Vermont, which has, you know, *zero* tennis opportunities. So I got shipped here."

"You like it, though? You wanted to come?"

"No. I cried every day for three months. I don't know that I like it, but I've accepted it. You know how before you play a match you have to *give* yourself to the match—to the outcome of the match, good or bad?" she said.

"Yeah." I knew exactly what she meant. Trent talked about it all the time. He called it surrendering to the game—to the lines, ball, racquet. Feel the game. Submit to the game. Trust. By surrendering to the game, the game freed a player mentally—to win. Zen. It was the only way to get into the zone. It felt like years since I'd been in the zone.

"Well, Bickford is like that. When I fought against

being here, I was miserable. No one cares if you're unhappy. It's not like at home, where your mom is going to come to your rescue. You have to get your butt out of bed and do the morning run, school, drills, matches, tournaments, homework, and then more drills anyway. And then drills, and drills, and then more drills . . ."

My head ached.

"Instead of being unhappy all the time, I figured I'd spare myself the mental breakdown and *give* myself to it, to Bickford, I mean. Now it doesn't bother me."

"Oh," I said.

"My mother says I've got to think of it as *me* using the *academy* instead of the academy using me."

Since she was being so honest, I decided to ask her the question that no player dared to ask another. This question was the black cloud, the fear, that hung over the heads of all on the junior circuit.

"Do you think you'll make it to the Tour, honestly?"

Katie stiffened and looked out the prison-type window. (I'd decided some of the academy's windows did actually resemble prison windows. I'd pointed this out to the Weak Link this morning over breakfast.)

"Do you?" I asked again.

"My dad thinks I will. He's paying serious cash for

me to be here . . . Who knows? College scholarship for sure. Free ride at college."

"But the Tour?" I asked impatiently.

"It's possible."

It was a lie. She knew she wouldn't. I knew she wouldn't before we'd played a set. Ranking too low, game too soft. Deep down, her father probably knew it, too.

What I didn't know was if I would make it to the Tour. If I couldn't beat Millicent, how could I beat a pro? But of one thing I was certain. No one at Bickford would buy me a Slurpee on the way home from a tournament or a Swiss flag because I had a crush on Roger Federer. Instead, they would make me run. Against my will.

"What about you?" she said quietly. "Think you'll make it?"

Her question melted as a stream of academy kids moseyed into her room, which, I could already tell, was some sort of meeting place for all of villa 2. They argued over U.S. Open statistics.

"They have a million ball people," some kid named Zane said. Bickford had many kids with ugly family names. No one questioned my name being Hall.

"They have two hundred and forty ball people, not millions, Zane," Katie said.

"Eight thousand," I said.

"Eight thousand what?" Zane asked.

"They use eight thousand towels at the U.S. Open. That's a lot of sweat."

The Bickford kids laughed.

Zane piped up. "Know how many spectators can watch in Arthur Ashe Stadium?"

"Twenty-three thousand," three other kids said in unison.

"Hence all the sweat," Katie said.

A man leaned in Katie's doorway. "Would you like thousands of people watching you in the stands someday, Hall?"

Everyone got quiet. I turned.

"Hall," Katie said, "this is Joseph Bickford. He founded and runs the academy."

The Bickford kids said hellos to him, waving. He smiled in return. No one had warned me that there was an actual Bickford *person* behind the name.

"Can I have a word or two with you, Hall? Out here?"

"Uh-huh."

I got off Katie's bed, brushed the potato chip crumbs off my lap, and joined Joseph Bickford in the hallway. His face was tanned and leathery-looking, his demeanor upbeat. A shiny watch covered his wrist.

"Hello," I said.

"Do you think you'd like thousands of people watching you in the stands of Arthur Ashe Stadium?" he asked again.

"Depends," I said. "Would I win or lose the match?"

He smiled so big his eyes disappeared into the lines in his face. "If you won?"

"Sure, who wouldn't?"

"What do you think about our academy?"

"It's a long way from Colorado."

"Yes, yes, it is," he said. His skin definitely looked like old leather. Like a cowboy's saddle or something.

"It's too far. I have a coach. Trent is my coach." I was glad my mom wasn't here or I would have had to be nice.

"You're a smart girl; let me ask you a question. Remember when Phil asked you to get to the ball quicker so you could execute a calm shot instead of an erratic one?"

"How did you know that?" I asked.

"I was watching you play."

"I didn't see you."

"I was there," he said. "After Phil told you that, you let the balls get behind you on purpose so you could run them down and test his theory. You took the chance of losing points in order to learn something new. Do you know how many of our other students would've done that?"

It seemed like a trick question. "No."

"Maybe five percent. Most of them are too busy with the vanity of easy shots to learn awkward ones."

"I still lost the set," I said. "She's better."

"The best of the best attend Bickford."

"In Colorado no one is better than me."

"This game is about dedication. You lost that set. Could've won but your mind wouldn't let you. You could win next time."

I wasn't sure what he was getting at.

"My coach says you've got to think there is no next time, otherwise you're giving yourself an excuse to lose."

"Your coach isn't playing the game. You are. I want to know what you think."

Silence.

"You're the one out on the court, aren't you?" he pressed. "I want to know what you think."

"I lost. Did you forget the part where I lost?"

He gazed down the hallway and back at me. "Why do you play tennis?"

I wasn't sure if I should tell him the truth. I wasn't

sure if I knew the truth anymore. "Because sometimes . . . well, I used to . . . I feel pretty when I play tennis." I waited to see if he'd laugh at me. He didn't. "People tell me I'm a champion."

"Yes. I've reviewed your records. You've got talent, but talent is irrelevant."

"What?" I asked.

"It's irrelevant. Everyone here is talented."

"Then why did you send for me?"

"Wanted to see if you have what it takes."

"Huh?"

"Talent is fine, but it's attitude that gets you through the tough times. People on the outside think tennis is just a game, but you know better, don't you, Hall?"

"I . . ."

"It's a hunger. Gets under your skin and doesn't let go. Winning the game is irrelevant. The battle is in you. Tennis pushes you, and you either push back or you accept defeat."

"Yes, yes . . ."

"True champions aren't afraid to lose. That's why they win," he said.

It was the truth and I knew it. My insides quaked. I couldn't speak. *True champions aren't afraid to lose. That's why they win.*

"I better get going." He shook my hand, his gleaming watch blinding me. "Nice meeting you." In an instant, he was gone.

"Hey, Hall!" Katie called from inside her room. "Which Grand Slam do you think is harder for a pro to win, Wimbledon or the French Open?"

• Chapter Nineteen •

My mom and I escaped from the Bickford campus and ate dinner alone. We barely spoke. Our minds were heavy. Later on, The Chin ushered us back to Bickford so we could view round-robin tournaments in progress.

I didn't feel like watching them play, so I excused myself. "Gotta find a bathroom," I said, and ditched them.

None of the dorm rooms had private bathrooms. In order to pee at midnight or otherwise an academy kid had to travel down the hall to the army-sized, latrine-type facilities. As I removed a piece of parsley from my teeth in the bathroom of villa 2, I listened to a girl have a breakdown.

"I hate it here," a Bickford girl said between sobs.

"It'll get better," her friend promised.

The girl wasn't buying it. Slumped over on the checkered tile, she was defeated. It was hard to tell the true origin of her stress. Could be from crazed tennis parents, from herself, or from Bickford. Maybe all three.

"It won't get better. My game is sucking more and more. I hate it here. I can't take one more year."

Her friend said, "Magda, come on, it's not that bad. You're just out of practice. Let's go hit a few balls, you'll feel better."

"Who are you kidding? It won't get better. Did you see Grendelli's face every time I served?" Magda asked her.

"But you almost beat Naomi Lennon just yesterday."

"That's nothing to brag about. Naomi Lennon is so bad she'll get the ax before Thanksgiving and you know it."

"It's Grendelli. He's an asshole. It's common knowledge. Don't let him get to you."

"I hate Coach Grendelli," Magda said.

"He's out to kill us all. Sadistic dictator is what he is," the other girl added.

"Coach Grendelli is a piece of shit and he can kiss my ass," Magda declared, agreeing.

"Shithead."

I was impressed with their level of hostility. They

seemed kind of poetic, talking trash in the girls' room while wearing matching Bickford Academy T's.

I was ready to introduce myself when Magda said, "I haven't won in a long time. I hate it here. They only like you if you win."

I shuddered.

They only like you if you win.

The hair at the nape of my neck stood up, and my heart was in my throat. It was the truth. For my whole life, Trent, Pete Graham, people at the country club, maybe even Janie Alessandro and Luke, they liked me because I won. Bickford would be no different. A tear ran down my cheek, then another, and more until I tasted salt on my lips. Terror overcame me.

The friend of the crying girl took a cigarette from her shorts pocket and lit it. She turned, gawking at me as if she just noticed me there. "What are you looking at?"

I didn't know what to say.

"I *said,* what are you looking at?"

Copping my own attitude: "Nothing, obviously."

She took a drag off the cigarette. "What are you going to do," she said, blowing the smoke my way, "tell on me?"

She failed to realize I was on her side. The poetry vanished. My heart beat like mad. I had to hold my own.

"I couldn't care less what you do."

"Bitch," she said.

The threat of a catfight in the ladics' room coaxed Magda from self-pity. She got between us, eyes still pink and swollen. "Come on, Sandrine. If you get written up for code again they'll expel you." She grabbed the cigarette, took a heaving drag, and flushed the evidence.

Magda pushed Sandrine toward the door. "She didn't mean it. Rough week. Bad week," Magda said, dismissing the drama. "Everything's cool."

Therein was the underbelly of Bickford Tennis Academy: glamorous on the outside, but malicious at its core.

They only like you if you win.

I'd read in my official *Bickford Academy Rules and Regulations Guidebook* (its thickness was that of a phone book) about code violations. Smoking, drinking, drug use, obscene language, inappropriate displays of affection, leaving campus without an official pass, fistfights, curfew violations, unsportsmanlike conduct, and all sorts of other, vaguer antisocial behavior were sure ways to get a violation. Three code violations equaled automatic expulsion, no exceptions.

Code violations seemed to be the equivalent of being grounded by one's parents, without the parents or the grounding. It didn't seem like either of those girls would last very long at Bickford.

Bickford was a planet all its own, free from outside,

non-tennis forces. I suspected its regulations were an attempt not to make good human beings out of its inhabitants but to simply remove anything that might detract from their tennis abilities.

This theme was so pervasive that even now, after being verbally assaulted by a nameless, faceless Bickford girl, my thoughts drifted not to revenge or puzzlement but to whether or not I could beat her on court. She was fifteen, at least—but I thought maybe I could beat her. I *wanted* to, at least. It was this thinking Bickford required—this thinking turned tennis talent into tennis legend.

Better, more, win. It never ended, only repeated. And I wondered, in an instant and passing thought, whether or not I was being brainwashed.

With my face against the wind, my spirit depleted, I walked outside to retrieve my mom. The brightly lit courts were packed with players of all ages, keeping honest score, playing hard rounds. My mom and The Chin were three courts over. Patiently she listened to Phil, her arms folded, stance calm. She adopted the same pose when one of my brothers brought home a D on a report card.

. . . *thump* . . .

My mom is a beautiful woman. Her mouth is placed

on her face in a way that makes it look like she's keeping a big secret. Tiny lines around her eyes crinkle when she laughs, making her even prettier. Often she complains that her fingernails don't look as good as they should. She votes for politicians who never win. I couldn't help but to want to please her. If only I knew how.

...*thump* ... *thump* ...

I leaned against the railing, closed my eyes, and listened to the tennis balls as they echoed from every direction. The sound a ball makes when it hits a racquet just right—that twang. It creeps into my soul. Frees me, that twang.

...*thump* ... *thump* ...

This trip was about me. Not for the me I am, but for the me I have the potential to *become.*

My dad slaved at two jobs so I could play a game.

Sacrifices made. Money spent. Weekends wasted. For what? For my tennis. Sacrifices for me so I could play a game. It wasn't a game anymore. A career now. Important now. He worked two jobs and didn't complain.

For what? For me, for tennis. *Don't disappoint us, please.* Never saying it aloud, never—don't want me to feel the pressure. Expectations exist. It's no one's fault. It's for something, right? Working two jobs for *something,* right? For me. For tennis. So I can win, conquer.

213

This is *for* something, right? Not a hobby, an opportunity. *Opportunity.* Don't deny the opportunity. What other parents would sacrifice like this? Money spent. Weekends wasted. Making sacrifices for *something,* right? ·

How could I tell them I didn't know how to win? They had such confidence in my game. In me. Couldn't disappoint them with the truth. *They only like you if you win*—I wanted to scream so that someone, anyone, would understand my predicament. What if I *can't* win anymore? What if I *never* win again? Who will I be then?

• Chapter Twenty •

"**E**ve has called you four times. Please remind your friends I'm not an answering machine," my mom said.

"Sorry." I picked up the phone and punched in Eve's magic code. My fingers were so used to dialing the pattern I did it without looking. The fact that Eve had called was nothing short of a miracle.

"I found one of your Prince racquets in my closet. Come and get it if you want it," she said.

"Hall," my mom screamed from downstairs, "Melissa is here!"

"Melissa's over. We'll see you in five minutes."

I joined Melissa in my driveway. She wore green shorts, a red shirt, and brown clogs—she was a rainbow of fashion disaster. Had Polly worn the outfit, it would've looked cool. On Melissa, it was ignorance.

"Nice outfit."

"Shut up, Hall."

"Where's Polly? She's not around?" I asked.

"She's at her interview thing," Melissa said. She held out a long rope of red licorice, offering me a bite.

I shook my head. "What interview thing?"

Melissa's face percolated like a coffeemaker. "For the school. Didn't she tell you?"

I'd only been gone three days—what the heck was going on? "What school, Melissa?" I practically screamed.

"Bruce's school. I was there when she got home from touring the campus, I know."

"Westland?" My mouth hung open in disbelief.

"Yeah," Melissa said. "Polly said it would be cool to go to school with Bruce. Maren is excited to go—I mean to have Polly go there."

I'd thought the whole Westland Prep thing was a cha-rade, just something Polly was dreaming about. She'd applied? Had an interview? But what about her hatred of math? A school like Westland was all about academic ex-cellence.

"That doesn't make any sense. Why would she do that to herself?" I asked.

"Don't know," Melissa said.

216

Complete faith in Melissa was something I didn't possess. Two summers ago, she ate a dog biscuit convinced it was a cookie. I'd wait and ask Polly. It had to be a mistake.

We received a cold reception from soft-spoken Ms. Jensen. The woman sighed heavily through the screen door, as if our mere existence had ruined her day. "Eve is in her room," she said, speaking in her telephone voice.

Melissa and I propped ourselves against a pink bedroom wall and watched blond Eve feverishly purge and reorganize her closet. "Here's your racquet," she said, shoving it at me, not looking at me.

"Don't tell me you're still mad at me, Eve," I said.

She threw a pile of jeans on the floor. "You can't ignore me and then suddenly remember we're friends when Polly isn't around. That's not friendship, that's stupid," she said.

Unaware of my problems with Eve, Melissa looked horrified. She swallowed her remaining bit of licorice in one big gulp.

"Eve—"

"*What?*" she said. "Why don't you go hang out with Polly? *She's* your best friend."

Ms. Jensen popped her head inside the doorway.

"We have to leave in twenty minutes to make the movie. Will you be ready?"

"Uh-huh," Eve said.

Ms. Jensen disappeared, and Eve glanced at us. "My mom and I are going to a movie at Cinemark IMAX, and then lunch after, so, you know, goodbye."

"Can I go, too?" Melissa asked.

"Sure, Melissa," Eve said while looking at me. "*You* can come if you want."

Ugh. My friendship with Eve was over without so much as a ceremony. Somehow I knew it wasn't her fault or mine. It wasn't Polly's fault, either—Eve and I had dissolved on our own. She was riding fast, first, in a different direction. I didn't want to play catch-up anymore. Still, I felt like crying. She wasn't just kicking me out of her room; she was kicking me out of her life. Ordinarily we would've shooed Melissa away and gone to the movies ourselves. Instead, I was discarded. I didn't know whether to be mad at myself for Eve's rejection or at Melissa for abandoning me.

"Well, bye, then," I said, sort of standing there like a fool.

Eve said nothing.

"Later," Melissa said.

I overheard Eve as I left. She wanted me to, I think.

"Hall's a loser. Thinks she's so great. 'Ooh, I'm a tennis player, yay for me,' " she mocked.

Not one to be mean, Melissa said nothing.

I slammed the Jensens' screen door against the frame as hard as I could, so it bounced several times before shutting. I walked up Wynkoop Drive alone, stray strands of sunshine melting fire into my skin.

My mom and dad were watching TV in the living room when I came home early from practicing serves. Actually, I didn't practice; I sat my butt on the court, thinking about Bickford, Polly and Westland, Eve . . .

"What's for dinner?"

"We're going out. To Fargo's," my mom said.

"Cool. Did Polly call?"

"No."

I grabbed my racquet and headed upstairs to call her.

"Hall, wait. We have great news," my mom said.

"What?"

"Great news," my dad said.

My heart sank. For the last three months "great news" seemed to be a code word for catastrophe.

My dad cleared his throat. "Joseph Bickford called from the academy. He was so pleased with your visit. He's offered you a full scholarship."

"Full scholarship," my mom sang. "Including room and board, coaching, admission to the private school, equipment, tournament fees, the whole deal."

"Full scholarship!" my dad repeated.

"As it turns out, they like girls that get upset and say four-letter words when they don't win," my mom said, in jest.

"Joseph Bickford thought you had a lot of spunk," my dad said.

"I didn't even know you spoke to Joseph Bickford," my mom said to me. "When was all this going on?"

"She probably had the place scouted out before you got out of the car, Vivian," my dad said. "Give the girl some credit. Heck, with those tennis shots she'll be having them pay *her* before long. She's better than those girls, and the coaches there know it—"

"Exactly." My mom beamed. "All her hard work has paid off."

"Stop it," I said.

My mom cocked her head, waiting.

"No!" I screamed.

They looked confused. "No what?" my mom said.

"I'm not going."

"What?" my dad said.

"Why on earth wouldn't you want to go?" my mom said.

"I'm not moving to Florida. *I'm not going to Bickford!* I'm not living at the academy, and you can't make me. *No!*" I screamed, and bolted out the door.

I ran and ran until my legs were numb and my lungs refused to hold air. Everything in me ached. I thought I might explode into tiny pieces and die right in the street.

They call tennis an individual sport, which is a total lie. How can it be a solitary sport when scores of people I've never met are disappointed, slighted, aggravated when I don't win? Win, win, win! For God's sake, girl, win!

They only like you if you win.

If tennis created me, then it could just as easily destroy me.

Later on, I reluctantly shoved my face into the heating vent. The conversation at the kitchen table was, as usual, about me.

Dad: "It's Bickford or it's nothing. Exactly what is the problem? Too easy for her, that's the problem. Got so much talent she doesn't appreciate it."

Mom: "Don't say that."

Dad: "Vivian, we're spending twenty thousand a year for what? For this to be a hobby? Nonsense. She can start a doll collection if that's all this is to her. Two years at the academy and we can turn pro."

221

Mom: "*We?* You mean *she.* I was twenty-five when I realized I held my future in my hands. Hall is thirteen. You need to back off."

Silence. Spoons stirred in coffee cups. I looked up from the vent. Michael and Brad leaned against the wall. Their quiet faces assessed the situation—they'd have to pick on me over the phone or something since I wouldn't be around anymore. Again, voices echoed up the vent.

Mom: "Give her a few days to sort it out, Frank. Admission day is August twenty-seventh. It's her decision."

Dad: "She better make the *right* decision."

Mom: "Her decision, Frank. This is her life."

Polly never called, but Luke did, asking me to meet him at his neighbors' house. I had to go.

• Chapter Twenty-one •

It was eight o'clock that night when I reached the iron-gated driveway. I crawled up, struggling to get my knees over the connecting stucco wall. I felt someone's hands on my butt.

"No, don't . . . Ouch!" I was pushed over, hard, and fell to the grass with a thud. "Hey!"

A giggle came from the other side of the wall.

"Luke?"

Grunts and groans peppered the air as the person attempted to scale the wall.

"Luke?"

"Ouch. Damn." Polly slithered across the top of the stucco ledge, her slender hands gripping it soundly so as not to fall. Tree leaves left her faceless for a moment. "No, it's not Luke. What, are you blind?" She leapt into the grass. "You're not the only one that can break into a house and swim. I've been *invited.*"

She looked crisp and lively, like she hadn't just sold her soul to endless math equations. Maybe Melissa was wrong.

I grabbed her arm. "It's still light out. Luke says to walk by the trees so no one will see. Polly . . . Melissa said that—"

"Shush," she said. "We're wasting time."

We made our way into the garden, where Luke and Bruce waited. "Here," Bruce said, handing the key to Polly, "you do the honors." She pushed her bangs from her eyes and wiggled the key into the slot. We entered slowly, Polly first.

Low voices fluttered from the far corner. Luke froze, eyes full of terror. Polly grinned, reveling in this.

"Is someone here?" Luke whispered to me.

I planted my feet, ready to run.

"Brandon," a high-pitched voice said, "someone's in here!"

Our eyes shot over to the furniture at the far end of the room. A guy's head peeked over the wicker love seat. Polly dug her nails into my flesh, pleased.

"Brandon," Luke whispered. "It's just me."

Stacey Kimberlin's perfect forehead popped up next to Brandon's. She groaned at the sight of us. No cutesy stories tonight, apparently. "Luke," she said, five decibels too loud, "you aren't supposed to bring people here! You are so busted! Get out!"

"Everybody calm down," Brandon said, standing.

"Luke, tell your stupid friends to go home! I'm not getting in trouble because of you again." She turned to Brandon. "Make his friends leave," she ordered.

Brandon laughed. He was good-looking and easy-going, his personality the opposite of Stacey's frenzied demeanor.

"Brandon! Make his friends leave!" Stacey said again.

"I think her head is going to start spinning," Polly whispered.

Brandon nodded to Luke. "Why don't you guys go to your house instead? Your parents went to dinner. They won't be back for a while."

"Sure, Brandon," Luke said.

The Greek God led us through the Kimberlin kitchen and up a back stairway to his room. To Polly's chagrin, he didn't provide us with a tour.

We piled onto his big unmade bed. Luke settled at

the head of his bed, me at the foot. Polly and Bruce sat close, between us.

I nudged Polly. "Melissa said you had an interview for Westland," I finally spat out.

Polly squealed. "I'll know in two days if I'm accepted. The dean of students loved me, says I'm Westland material."

"Sweet," Bruce said.

So it was true.

"I recited part of Shakespeare's *Romeo and Juliet.* The woman almost fell out of her chair."

"Yeah, they're fond of brownnosers at Westland," Luke said. "Just stay away from the whipped cream."

Bruce laughed. Polly ignored him.

"Maren found out they offer automatic financial aid to single-parent families. With the aid it ends up costing less than the academic camps I go to all year," she explained.

"Don't do it," Luke said. "Run fast, run far. That's all I need at Westland, one more ass kisser making me look bad."

"She plans on running for class president," Bruce said.

"Oh great," Luke said.

"They let you take fencing in gym class," Polly said, speaking only to me, fed up with their lack of sincerity.

"They *let* you go to detention if you fail to report to study hall. Did the dean of students tell you about that?" Luke inquired.

"Bruce, will you please tell your friend to shut up? He's making me sick," Polly said.

"Luke, shut up or she's gonna puke all over your bed."

"It won't be pretty," I said, joining in, biding my time until I could squire Polly away and ask what was going on.

The Greek God rolled his eyes.

Polly continued torturing Bruce with her concerns. She fired questions with calculated rhythm. I was afraid to interrupt for fear she'd slug me.

"Do you always have to wear uniforms? . . . What are the teachers like? . . . What time do morning classes start? . . . How long are holiday breaks? . . ."

I tuned out Bruce's answers and gazed at the Greek God's belongings. His room was a mess: clothes and sports equipment covered the floor. And then I zeroed in on something. Trent's Roger Maris baseball, in its plastic case, sat on Luke's bookshelf! My belly turned over and over again as I stared at it in disbelief.

What had he done? I weighed my relationships with Trent and the Greek God mentally. Which one deserved my loyalty? Luke was good for kissing, but Coach was good for my game.

I would rather eat dirt than tell Coach of the

thievery—Coach was always on my side. When he drove me to tournaments he didn't complain about the traffic. If my cherry Slurpee happened to spill in his car, he never sighed or rolled his eyes or anything. When he threatened to make me run sprints it was because he *liked* me. He appreciated the way I hit a Penn ball over a three-foot-high net. He took pride in his stupid baseball. Why shouldn't he? It was his.

Yet I knew Luke hadn't taken it to hurt me. To Luke it was probably just another exciting event, like sneaking into the pool house, flipping off that guy at the 7-Eleven, or putting whipped cream on a car.

But still, it was *Coach's* ball. I had to get away and clear my head. "Luke, where's the bathroom?"

"Across from the study," he said.

"I'll go with you." Polly jumped up.

I knew she would. After mistakenly opening a linen closet, we managed to find it.

She squealed. "Look at the toilet!"

It was old-fashioned-looking. The tank was five feet above the seat and a pull chain caused it to flush. The air freshener smelled like oranges. She sat on the marble floor while I peed.

"Brandon is cute, huh?" she said.

"Did you see the baseball? Trent's baseball was on Luke's bookshelf. He stole it."

"From the club? Wow!"

"I'm an accessory to a crime!" I said, and groaned. "Luke doesn't deserve such a great forehead."

"What?"

"Never mind."

I flushed the toilet and joined Polly on the marble floor. My heart was heavy: partly about the baseball, and partly about her.

"Hall, you told me Luke swiped that candy bar, didn't you? You shouldn't be that stunned."

"But this is my coach, Janie."

"First you call me Luke, now I'm Janie? Who the heck is Janie?"

"She was—she is—a friend of mine, from tennis. I guess you remind me of her."

"I could wear a name tag, if you want."

"That won't be necessary."

"You sure? Maybe you need glasses. Then I can call you Four Eyes. Or Four, for short." She giggled.

"Polly?"

"Yes, Four?"

"I'm being serious."

She saluted me as if I was her captain. "Yes, Four. We must be serious. Go ahead."

Just when I thought I'd pinpointed who she was, she again wiggled free of my theories and became something else entirely. First she was a math genius who claimed we were twins, then a parade director at my practice court, a boa-wearing chorus girl, an angel sent by Janie to save me, and finally a ghost sent by Janie to taunt me. And right now I felt I didn't know her at all.

"Polly," I said quietly, "why are you applying to Westland? You'll be in math up to your eyeballs. You know that, right?"

Energy drained from her face.

"You're going to Westland on *purpose!*" I accused.

Her fingers tapped on the marble floor. One, two, three . . . one, two, three . . .

"Polly?"

She didn't turn from my eyes. "Because I like Bruce," she finally said. "That's why. Come on, they're waiting. Let's have fun."

I lay on the floor, pressing my cheek to the cool marble. It was silky smooth and surprisingly dirt-free. "There is no fun. I hate fun."

Polly rested her hand on my head. "What's wrong?"

I wanted to tell her about Bickford, about how my life was over, about how I couldn't manage to hit a damn yellow ball over a net. I wanted to smack her for pretending her academic pressure equaled my tennis stress. It was such a betrayal. Her agony was clearly not that overwhelming, not if it could be brushed aside so easily for the likes of Bruce Weissman. "Nothing's wrong," I said.

"So let's go," she said, opening the door.

It wasn't Polly and me against some big force. It was me. I was all alone.

Quieted, we walked to Luke's room.

"What, you guys fall in?" Bruce asked.

I sidled up to Luke. I rested my hand on his back for a moment and then dug my fingernails into his shoulder and watched him flinch, wondering how I was going to get Coach's baseball returned. Then I ran my knuckle down his backbone as hard as I could.

Luke shrieked like a girl. "I'd like to keep my spine if you don't mind."

The Kimberlins' garage door opened, rattling. Luke was stricken. "That's my parents, they're home early."

Bruce bolted up, scrambling.

"We'll go out the back," I said to Polly.

"You have to or I'll get grounded," Luke said, waving for us to hustle.

Polly, Bruce, and I escaped, charging down the hall.

• Chapter
Twenty-two •

I found Trent in his office, doing paperwork. He was abruptly excited, joy-filled, like a kid at a birthday party. Cheer swept his face, and as always, I had to restrain myself from touching my fingers to his temple. Damn, I wanted some of that cheer. Part of him probably wished *he* was the player and the academy had brought *him* to Florida. He loved the game that much.

"So, are you going to tell me about Bickford? How was the place?"

My mom hadn't told Trent the news of my Bickford scholarship—said it was my responsibility. It was hard enough to look at the merriment on his face; if I told him the news, he'd get ecstatic and I'd start crying or something.

"Hall? How was the place?"

I tried to be polite. "This one girl, Millicent, she could play for sure. Turning pro soon. Mopped up the court with me."

"You could use a good beating on court. Keeps you motivated."

"Yeah. I guess."

"They churn out some top players. Forget about your USTA ranking—you'll get some real experience playing foreign tournaments. Rack up an international ranking in no time."

"I know."

"It's a good program—good results."

"So why don't you go there?" I spat.

He didn't catch it. "What were the grounds like?"

I shifted my weight from one foot to the other and remained mute. Fate taunted me, ridiculed me. The back of my neck burned. I felt like Coach was trying to get rid of me or something.

"Hall? The grounds? I meant to have you take some pictures so that Annie and I could see—"

"Who cares about the grounds?" My shrill voice blindsided him. "Haven't you got anything better to do than worry about my tennis game?"

"Hall, what are—"

"Seriously, is that what you do all day? Figure out

233

how to make me a star in order to make yourself look good? Teach me the game so you can have a claim on me along with everyone else? I can't stand you."

Coach studied the cap of his pen, dulled by my outburst. A long silence ensued.

"I've been your coach since you were nine."

I said nothing.

"I want nothing but for you to have as much joy playing tennis as people have watching you play. The crowd *anticipates* you, Hall. You step on the court, and there is *respect*. You don't see it because you're focused on the task at hand, but I see it."

"I'm not in the mood for one of your stupid pep talks."

He placed his hand on his shaved scalp as if to comfort himself. By questioning his intentions, I'd damaged him somehow. And it felt good. Nobody understood me.

I looked at a framed picture on his desk. It was of the two of us at the Junior Orange Bowl last year. I'd just won. The smile on his face was bigger than the one on mine. I was a selfish, selfish girl—stomping on his cheer after all he'd done for me—and I didn't care.

I wanted to hurt him. Wanted to slug him or tip his chair over and watch him fall on his ass. I wanted to make him cry so he'd know how I'd felt all summer, pounding balls over a net, unable to hear his voice, afraid.

Coach pushed aside his papers, mulling my expression. "Braxton?" he said, looking perplexed.

My heart crumbled; big hunks of it melted into the bottom of my shoes. I was the most awful girl in the whole world.

"I understand," he said.

I shook my head. "You couldn't possibly."

"This has nothing to do with tennis. You can be weak, or you can stand up and be the woman you know how to be. It's your choice. Do what you have to do." His hand was glued to his head. Fingers as big as sausages. "No one wants to hear you complain about being gifted. I didn't give you wings so you could live in a cage."

"So I'm a bird now?"

"You can fly, Hall. As sure as I'm sitting here, you can fly."

I ran my hand over his thick mahogany desk. The wood was far smoother than my skin. My naked palm was the callused and rough hand of a workman or lumberjack. For weeks now, no matter what I was doing—eating a grapefruit, brushing my teeth, making my bed—it felt like I had my favorite stick in my grip. It wasn't a racquet anymore; it was an extension of my arm. Tennis was so infused in me I had no clue where it stopped and I started.

Trent navigated us into safer waters. "The grounds?" he said for the third time. "What were they like?"

The man never let up. I was too exhausted to fight. "Uncle," I said.

"Excuse me?"

"Nothing." There was no reasoning with him. "Well, let's see, um . . . the courts were spotless. Clay, hard court, grass too. They have an in-house rehabilitation center."

"Uh-huh, uh-huh. Have they called since you've been back? I tried contacting them, but it seems every-one of importance is at a tournament in Boca Raton. Did they say they'd stay in touch?"

"I don't know," I lied. "Haven't heard from them." I got quiet. "Don't you want to be my coach anymore? Trent? Why can't you be my coach?"

Trent swallowed hard. His eyes got watery, though a tear didn't dare fall. "They can take you places I can't. We don't even have grass courts to practice on, much less clay. You'll flourish in their environment."

"No, Coach, no—"

"I'll be your coach in here," he said, thumping his heart. "Always."

He looked as if he might hug me, but it wasn't in his nature to go around hugging people. Without thinking, I touched my fingers to his temple and felt that fine cheer beneath his skin. He didn't mind.

"You're a fantastic person, Hall. Don't let anyone tell you different."

"They said I have a good coach," I said weakly.

Trent folded his large arms and bellowed out a chuckle. "*Only* good? You set them straight, right? Told them I'm the *best,* didn't you?"

"Oh, Coach."

A country club employee popped his head into the office, knocking on the door once to get Trent's attention. "I asked Nelson if he's seen it, but he swears he hasn't. Bet one of those thug lifeguards swiped it as a joke."

"Probably. That's what I get for bragging about it all the time. It'll turn up. Thanks for asking Nelson, though," Trent said.

"No problem," the guy said, waving a quick good-bye.

"What's that about?"

"My baseball is missing—probably Finnegan from bookkeeping, now that I think about it. The guy's a prankster, thinks he's a comedian."

His missing baseball. Ugh.

Trent shuffled papers. "Let's get on the court."

I just couldn't. "Nah, I don't feel well. I'm gonna call my mom to pick me up."

"There's work to be done. You can't run from tennis, Hall. Tennis isn't the enemy. You run *to* tennis, not away."

"You can't tell me what to do," I said.

He looked me in the eye. "You're right, I can't. But I'll see you on court in ten minutes anyway."

In the deserted locker room, I sat on the sink counter and stared at my reflection in the mirror. I was an average girl: not pretty, not ugly. Hair the color of mud, limbs thin and lanky. A wisp of a girl, as my mom often says. Only my tennis racquet hinted at splendor.

Trent's voice was gone forever. Of this I was certain. It troubled me every second of the day.

I had to find a new way.

Nothing turned out like I planned. I doubted Eve would ever speak to me again. At the moment, Luke was a fraud. Polly wrongly claimed we were twins. But she was bullied into achieving something she never wanted—just like Janie—and it had nothing to do with me. No one forced me to play tennis. I played for myself. Always had. Sure, expectations were there, everywhere. But I chose this game.

I wanted this.

I arranged my zinc oxide containers in front of me like a paint set. Dipping my finger into the white, I covered my nose until no skin showed through. Like a football player, I made one line below each eye.

With purple zinc, I placed six perfect dots above my eyebrows and one on my chin. Yellow lines ran down my cheeks. My reflection transformed. I couldn't see my stick limbs or mud-colored hair. Couldn't tell if I was pretty. All I saw was a warrior. Not someone's daughter. Not someone's friend. An Amazon armed with a racquet. A girl who played to win.

As I exited the locker room something inside me broke. Joseph Bickford's words besieged my mind . . . *The battle is in you. True champions aren't afraid to lose. That's why they win . . .*

I needed tennis. It was a lie to pretend I didn't.

People call me a champion, a warrior. They're wrong. I'd trusted Trent's voice would make me win instead of allowing myself to become a real champion.

True champions aren't afraid to lose.

Tennis pushes: push back or accept defeat.

I wanted to love this game again.

The squeaking gate of court 3 announced my arrival. Trent squinted, not knowing what to make of the warrior paint. He said nothing. I motioned for Skittish Helper Guy to start the ball machines. "Turn them both on. Put the levers on high."

"With two it'll be too fast. Won't stand a chance," Skittish Helper Guy said.

"Put the levers on high," I said again.

He looked to Trent.

Trent stared at the battle paint on my face. "Do what she wants," he said. Intrigued, he sat down, his bellowing voice silenced.

Penn balls launched from the mouths of the machines. Rhythmically. One after the other. Hard. With wicked minds. Evil intentions. Intimidating me. Taunting, spitting. Screaming, *You can't hit me . . .*

But I can. I can. I will. I missed one, then two. A third cleared the fence.

. . . you can't hit me . . .

But I will. Can. I closed my eyes for a second, focusing. Four, five, six balls passed. Looking around hungrily, I defied anyone to say a word.

Objects and people around me blurred, sounds ceased. Heartbeats thundered in my chest. The zone was near. I had the choice. I could give into the pressure and have a breakdown, right here on the court like Janie Alessandro. Insanity would be the easy way out. Or I could hit the hell out of this next ball, go to Bickford, and give myself to tennis.

"I am Holloway Braxton, and I play to win."

"What?" Skittish Helper Guy hollered.

I snapped myself further into a deep focus. My guts burned, gurgled. A great rumble of water, a river, sprang forth in my belly, waking me, shaking me, scalding my insides.

The machine released a ball from its mouth. Spinning, spinning, it sailed over the net, spinning, spinning. I ran across court, brought my racquet back . . .

Slam the ball, a voice said. *You know how to do this. This is easy.*

It wasn't Trent's voice inside my head, it was *mine.*

Slam the ball, my voice demanded. *Push, try . . . slam the ball . . .*

The court opened.

My *world* opened.

I swung with all my might. The blur of yellow, smacked senseless by my racquet, flew over the net, deep to the left corner, for a winner.

It was beautiful. My God, the beauty.

"Yes!" I screamed. "Perfection."

I hit another ball. And another. On the line. In the corner. Backhand. Forehand. Slice. Crosscourt. Down the line. Overhead. Volley. Chip and charge. Attack the net. Again. Again. Zen. Win!

I turned to Trent. Speechless, he clapped ferociously as he laughed and laughed.

I put my hands to my knees, catching my breath. I couldn't put it off any longer. I'd avoided it all summer. It was time. "Hey, Coach. Want to go on a field trip?"

He got confused, glanced at his watch. "We're not done yet."

"I'm not asking, Coach. I'm telling."

He stared at me from across court, alerted to the moment, alerted to my freedom, *alerted.* He nodded. "OK, Braxton, let's go."

• Chapter
Twenty-three •

It felt strange being in Coach's SUV without Annie in the passenger seat.

"All right. Where to?" Coach said.

"To get your baseball back."

He stopped fumbling with his keys and looked me square in the eyes. I was ashamed it had taken me this long; I didn't need his disappointed gaze, too. "Coach, this will be easier if you just don't ask."

Bewilderment slid across his face. "You, Braxton?"

"I didn't do it! What would I want with your baseball? But I know who has it." I shuddered. Nothing about getting that baseball back was going to be easy. But I couldn't let Luke do that to Coach. I just couldn't. "Do you know how to get to Naples Drive?"

*   *   *

Miraculously, Coach promised to wait in the SUV. He didn't have a choice; the iron gate was locked. He helped ease me over the wall while lecturing me on the dangers. Then he stood, facing me, fists wrapped around the iron bars, stuck in his own helpless prison. "Hall, if they don't want to give it back to you, you come get me. *I'll* make them give it back."

"Don't worry, Coach, I'm getting that ball!" I declared.

I took off, running up the driveway, looking back once. Coach paced like a bull on the other side of the gate. I'd have to do this quick. He looked three seconds away from reneging on the deal, ramming his SUV through the gate, and charging up the Kimberlin driveway.

Luke answered the door, surprised. "What are you doing here, Holloway?" He stared at my face, not my eyes.

"I need that baseball, Luke," I said. I didn't accuse him, I wasn't condescending. It almost didn't matter why he took it. Maybe he did it because he couldn't stand up to his friends and be on the chess team. Maybe he was impulsive. Or maybe he really was a thief. I didn't know. And I didn't have time to care.

I looked back. No sign of Trent yet, but he wasn't going to wait long.

"You scaled the gate by yourself?"

"My coach helped."

"Do you want to come in? Um, we can't swim or anything today. Stacey's over there with her boyfriend. What's wrong with your face?"

"Luke, I need that baseball back."

"Yeah, but, your face is . . ."

"I'm mad. That's what's wrong with my face."

I caught his eyes. He looked down for a second. Ashamed? Embarrassed? I wasn't sure.

"I know you took it. It's my coach's ball, Luke. He's going to come up here, and if he does, I don't even want to know what's going to happen."

"Who cares? It's a baseball. He can't prove it was his. He can get another one."

"Luke, you don't understand. I'm doing you a favor. If Coach knows your name, he'll have your membership to the club revoked."

"I can't believe you, Holloway!" he spat, eyes wild, chest heaving. "Did you *tell* him I took it?"

He moved, blocking the doorway. From me. Like I was the enemy. That was his choice, making me the enemy, not mine. Blood sped through my veins.

"This isn't like the candy bar at 7-Eleven, Luke—I saw you steal that, too. Coach paid a lot of money for that ball, but it wouldn't matter if he'd paid only a dollar for it, it's his! Give it back."

He snapped his head up, angry. "Make me."

What? *Make me?* Where was my apology? I wanted a confession, a promise it'd never happen again, some remorse! *Make me?* Something inside my head went *click*.

Did I need, want, crave someone who said, *Make me?*

I salivated like a hungry mutt of a dog. I couldn't have stopped myself if I wanted to—I thrust my hands out and shoved him, hard. His back slammed into the door. His footing went awry. *Thud.* His ass hit the floor. "Hey!" he hollered.

I ran up the back stairway—the only way I knew how to get to Luke's room—passed two doors, and flung myself into his room, looking, hunting, searching. I slapped my pulsating paws on the plastic case and just as quickly sprinted back down the stairs.

Face sour, body reeling, forehead perfect, he stood where I'd left him. He didn't try to stop me this time.

"Made you," I said, and barreled past. It seemed like four steps, maybe fifty-four, pounding down his driveway.

"Holloway!" Luke yelled.

I didn't answer. Didn't even turn my head.

"What's the matter with you? Give it back!" Luke hollered.

Trent came into focus. His SUV door opened and he popped out, his features gaining cheer. A mixture of sun and tree shadows spilled across his stout body. His relieved sigh hit the air, piercing it, piercing me, and I knew I'd done the right thing.

He steered with one hand and held on to the plastic case with his other, protecting it as if it was a child.

"Hall . . ."

"Don't ask, Coach. Please, don't ask."

He scoffed. Then laughed.

"Should've seen yourself fly down that driveway. Never seen you run that fast voluntarily. Remember that feeling and do it on court, would you?"

For some reason that struck me. "Will do, Coach."

"Where to now?" he said, suddenly sounding up for anything.

I looked out the window. The afternoon was still young. "To Wellsprings," I said. "To see Janie."

Coach's eyes stayed on the road. His nostrils flared the slightest bit. He nodded and said nothing.

Trent walked me in. Wellsprings Mental Health Facility wasn't as scary as I imagined. A huge grassy lawn spread off its side, with large windows for a full view of it. The receptionist considered me carefully, like I might be a resident, not a visitor. But when she heard who we were there to see, she smiled. "Janie," the woman said. "We love Janie. She's over there, waiting for her mom to pick her up; they're going out for dinner." She pointed to the furniture groupings in front of the windows.

"She can leave?" I asked.

"She's out for good next week," Trent said. "They just had to get her medication dosage right."

Coach and I walked past a row of ferns. He stopped. "Alessandro!" he called.

Janie looked up from the magazine she was reading and turned. Recognizing me, she shook her head wryly. She wasn't in a straitjacket or anything. She wore normal clothes.

Coach nudged me. "I'm going to get some air."

I nodded. That was good of him. He used to hang back sometimes when Janie and I practiced together—take himself out of the equation and leave us to our ambitions. It was right of him to do that, and this.

My heart ticked, askew. A lump of regret choked my throat. I hoped I wasn't going to cry and make a blubbering fool of myself. Janie took a step toward me. That was all I needed. That killed me. I took two for every one of hers, and we met in front of a potted ficus tree. I grabbed her and hugged her hard. "I should've come before now," I whispered in her ear. "I'm so sorry."

Her thick mane of dark brown hair smelled like strawberries from her brand of shampoo. It always had. I'd forgotten that.

She peeled me off her and backed up so I could witness her mug fill with pretend disgust. "You should be," she said. "Took you long enough."

I kept hold of her shoulder. I didn't want her to slip from my grasp. I had to know something, anything, everything she could tell me. Her coloring was a little off—paler—and she was quieter. Yes, quieter, but she was Janie again. Not the least bit deranged, not like that day on the court. She was *Janie.*

We chose a leather couch that faced the sprawling grass beyond the windows. Odd ugly purple and green pillows covered the brown leather.

"I'm loving the decor. No wonder these people are crazy," I said. Then I winced. I shouldn't have said that—"crazy." Was she crazy? Still? The word "crazy" was dismissive. It was more complicated than that. It was expectation, pressure, winning.

Janie held me in her sights, then motioned to the pillows. "These are Wimbledon colors, girl, bite your tongue."

Yes, it was Janie. *She was back.* I did bite my tongue—to keep myself from crying with joy.

"So they are."

We had a view of Trent outside. He walked around aimlessly on the endless lawn. It didn't look like he could see us, because of the glare on the windows, but we could see him fine.

"Speaking of tennis," Janie said, "Coach told me you won the Cherry Creek Invitational."

"He did?"

"That's two years in a row, Hall."

Hmmm. She didn't seem to mind talking about it. "Yeah, but you don't know how bad I sucked. You wouldn't have believed it. Coach went through five pens taking notes. He ran out of ink before I ran out of mistakes. Then he made me write a sportsmanship essay, *that's* how bad I sucked."

"Ouch. Topic?"

I grinned stupidly at that—*Ouch. Topic?* She leaned forward as she spoke. Face paler. Voice a notch quieter. But her eagerness, the summary of her whole persona, was intact. "U.S. Open quarterfinal match between Agassi and Sampras," I said.

"Oh, excellent choice!"

"It *is* an awesome match," I acknowledged.

Using the tip of her pinkie finger, she touched my chin and displayed the resulting purple smudge on her finger. "You just come from practice?"

Zinc oxide still covered my face. Ugh! No wonder Luke had kept asking about my face and the receptionist had stared. Nothing unusual to Janie, though.

I missed her right then, even though she sat within arm's length. I missed her for what a god-awful desperate summer it had been—everyone asking me questions about tennis but never truly understanding my answers. Janie understood. But was she really OK? How could she be without tennis? Didn't she ache without it?

"Check him out," she said, pointing to Coach.

Pigeons swarmed him for some reason—literally, from every direction. Trent appeared to panic at this. He looked around to see if anyone was watching. No one else was on the grounds, and it was clear he didn't know we could see him. He shuffled his feet, kicking at a couple of them. Soft at first, then harder. It was a sitcom, fierce Coach trying to shoo those plump birds. They weren't going.

Janie busted up laughing. Hard. Out of the corner of my eye I made a mental outline of the shape of her cheeks—Polly's cheeks, the cheeks that haunted my summer.

"Think we should help him?" she asked. And busted up again. That laugh. That laugh was a hundred percent Janie. A cackle, really. A bottomless, throaty cackle. Classic Janie. Her pain was deep, and the laugh matched it, balanced it.

"I met your twin," I said. "They say everyone has one."

"Is she a tennis star?"

"No, math whiz."

Janie made a face. "Ew, ick."

"No kidding."

She placed a green pillow on her lap. We couldn't keep our eyes off Coach. He was pretty much getting dive-bombed by pigeons. They were coming at his head. He was sort of running from them, that big man.

I felt Janie's gaze on me. "I think he's afraid of them," I said.

"I don't," she said, voice low.

I turned to her. "Hmmm?"

"I don't miss it—tennis," she said. "Isn't that why you're here? Why you didn't come before? I don't miss it, Hall. Miss Coach sometimes. You. But not the game. I didn't have the head for it. I had the skills. It's not the same thing. You know it's not," she said quietly.

I wasn't about to lie to her. "I know it's not," I said.

"I was just so terrified of losing, not just choking during a match, but losing . . . myself, I guess . . . my mind shut down, that's all."

I nodded. Whatever I'd suffered this summer, she'd suffered worse. So much worse. I felt selfish.

"My parents are getting divorced," she announced.

"Oh, Janie . . ."

"Can you believe my dad still wants me on the pro circuit after all this? My mom said over her dead body, thus the divorce."

"He always was a jackass," I said.

Again, the laugh. The cackle. *But what about tennis?* I wondered. *Says she doesn't miss it, but how could she not?* Then I knew. Janie didn't miss it. *I would.* I exhaled, exhausted suddenly.

She glanced at her watch. "You're finally here, and now I have to tell you to go away," she said. "My mom will be pulling up in about thirty seconds—we're going to go eat. I gotta go grab my purse."

I nodded. We stood and hugged our goodbyes. I walked away a few feet and turned back. She hadn't moved. My belly quaked. I had to tell her. I didn't want her hearing it from Coach later on. "Janie, I'm going to Bickford Tennis Academy," I said.

She stiffened, looked out the windows at Coach,

then back at me. Something pushed into her face—no, into *her.* Relief, I think. Had to be. Relief it was me, not her, going to Bickford. She nodded slowly. Using the smear of purple zinc on her fingertip, she made a line down her chin, somehow both approving of me and separating us forever.

"Of course you are, Hall. Of course you are," she said, like she knew it all along.

I climbed back into Coach's SUV and shut the door. Restlessness bounced off Coach in waves. He had things to say. I knew he did. But he waited for me to speak.

"I just wanted Janie to still play tennis, Coach. I wanted her to be OK and play tennis."

"I did, too, Hall," he said softly. "More than you know."

He looked fragile admitting that. We were the same, Coach and me. Warriors: hard on the outside but with secret soft centers.

"I was worried I'd end up like her," I said, looking out the window.

"But you won't. You're not her."

"I believe it now," I said. "I believe it."

Coach tipped his head to me. It was settled.

The engine revved. He turned the air-conditioning on full blast and paused, adjusting the vents.

Something still nagged at me, and I needed an answer. "Coach, remember how you didn't want any boys watching my practice?"

He kept quiet.

"Do you think I have to give up boys to play tennis?"

He writhed under his seat belt, considering it.

"Coach?"

"Can't you just have a crush on Roger Federer?" he said. "From far away?"

"But that's not fair. I don't even know Roger Federer."

Coach sighed heavily. Giving in. So unlike him. "No, I guess that wouldn't be fair. Can't you at least like a boy who plays tennis? Somebody who won't distract you from the game?"

I thought of the boys at Bickford—the ones on the group run, with tanned legs and excellent foreheads. I laughed at myself. Out loud. Why hadn't I thought of that before? Luke Kimberlin wasn't the only hot boy in the world. "Well, yeah, I could like a tennis player," I said.

"If someone doesn't respect your tennis, they don't respect you."

"Got it, Coach."

"Good. Can we go back to the club now, Braxton? Are all your errands done?"

"Sure, Coach."

Coach jolted the SUV into gear and pulled out of the parking lot. I wanted to tell him about Bickford, about my scholarship, about my future. About the new, perfect voice in my glorious head. But I decided to wait one more day; otherwise he'd sideline practice to hear the details. Right now I needed to get back on court. And play.

• Chapter
Twenty-four •

I wrote Trent a postcard after my first hellish week at Bickford Tennis Academy to let him know I was still alive, that I'd survived so far. Sensing my homesickness, he called immediately, the sound of his booming voice making me laugh.

Both Annie and my mom send me a continual stream of care packages, and I know that they do care.

Janie and I talk on the phone about everything *except* tennis. I wrote Eve a handful of letters but never got a response. Friendships aren't forever. I wish her well. Melissa remains a fixture in the neighborhood, and I read her letters with amusement. Polly and I made a pact to stay friends. I'm not sure how long it will last; our lives are so different now. Things change. People change. From what I hear, she rules the halls of Westland Prep, just like she planned. She tells me the Greek God spends the majority of his free time in detention. I don't miss his forehead as much as I thought I would.

The Dead Grandpa Bonus Fund is getting some use after all, in the form of airplane tickets to the swampy Florida heat. Who would have thought I'd stand in an airport anxiously awaiting my brothers? I can hardly believe it myself.

At some point, I guess everyone has to decide what's important to them. There are no right or wrong answers. Janie was brave to decide she didn't have the head for tennis. Polly spent a summer fighting against math, only to invite it into her life for the chance to go to school with Bruce. While Luke chose his friends over chess, Eve and I decided our friendship wasn't worth our time anymore.

But one thing is true and constant: anything that matters in life, that's pure, is going to be a hassle. It's going to be hard. Maybe even hurt. I don't know why, it just is. Getting to Bickford Tennis Academy isn't the end of my challenges but the beginning. It's complicated here at times, but I'm pushing aside expectations. It's going well. I'm feeling good.

Tennis matters to me. It's who I am. It's what I do.

I'm willing to put up with the hassle.

Besides, I'm one of the lucky few who got assigned a single room. And it isn't true what that girl said in the bathroom of villa 2 that day: they still like me even when I *don't* win. I lost a couple of times on purpose just to make sure.

• Acknowledgments •

Many thanks to my parents, Shirley and Robert Clippinger, the most excellent people I will ever know. Somehow "thank you" doesn't say enough.

Much appreciation goes out to my huge family: Linda, Ken, Chris, and Josh McDaniel; Jennifer, Travis, and Katie Tillett; David, Vickie, Kyle, and Kevin Clippinger; Sue, Len, and Kelly Meyer; Jimmy and Jeff Kemp; Ron, Kelly, and Witney Clippinger; and Don, Rochelle, Jade, Lindsay, and Tristan Clippinger. Winners, every one of them.

With special thanks to Julie Rey for the million days of my childhood that I walked down Wynkoop Drive to get to her front door.

Also to Glen Agritelley for his connections and to Chris Wade, the athletic director at T Bar M Racquet Club, and Karla Jones, USTA Player Development.

And thanks to Sherrill Oglevie, my captive audience and cheerleader, at Sherrill's Shears.

And last but not least, much gratitude to my enthusiastic agent, Steven Chudney, and to my intrepid editor, Erin Clarke, for her encouragement and guidance.